Also by Wendy Wan-Long Shang

The Great Wall of Lucy Wu

The Way Home Looks Now

The Secret Battle of Evan Pao

with Madelyn Rosenberg

This Is Just a Test

Not Your All-American Girl

Bubble Trouble

By Wendy Wan-Long Shang

Scholastic Press / New York

Library of Congress Cataloging-in-Publication Data available

Names: Shang, Wendy Wan Long, author.
Title: Bubble trouble / by Wendy Wan-Long Shang.
Description: First edition. | New York : Scholastic Press, an imprint of Scholastic Inc., 2023. | Audience: Ages 8–12. | Audience: Grades 4–6. | Summary: Chloe loves musicals and is desperate to go on the class trip to Broadway, but since her mother died money has been tight, and her father's zany inventions are not selling—so with the help of her best friend Sabrina Chloe comes up with a way to make some money by making and selling boba tea.
Identifiers: LCCN 2022035150 | ISBN 9781338802146 (hardcover) | ISBN 9781338802153 (ebook)
Subjects: LCSH: Fathers and daughters—Juvenile fiction. | Money-making projects for children—Juvenile fiction. | Best friends—Juvenile fiction. | Friendship—Juvenile fiction. | Chinese Americans—Juvenile fiction. | CYAC: Fathers and daughters—Fiction. | Moneymaking projects—Fiction. | Best friends—Fiction. | Friendship—Fiction. | Chinese Americans—Fiction. | BISAC: JUVENILE FICTION / Family / General (see also headings under Social Themes) | JUVENILE FICTION / Social Themes / Friendship | LCGFT: Novels.
Classification: LCC PZ7.S52833 Bu 2023 | DDC 813.6 [Fic]—dc23/eng/20220809
LC record available at https://lccn.loc.gov/2022035150

10 9 8 7 6 5 4 3 2 1   23 24 25 26 27

Printed in Italy   183

First edition, July 2023

Book design by Stephanie Yang

To my boba lovers–
Matthew, Jason, and Kate

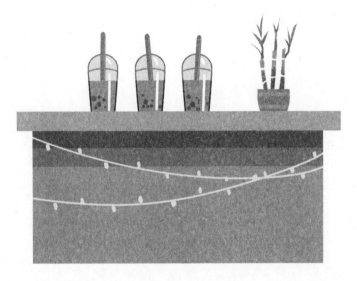

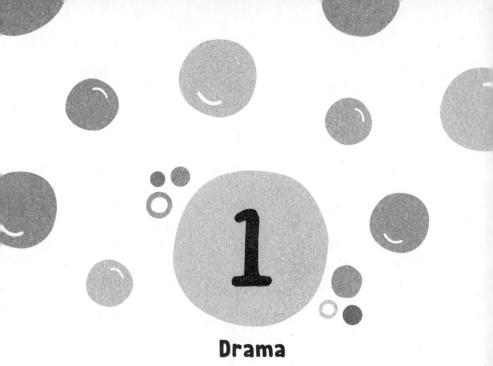

Drama

Is it possible to fail drama, even when you're trying your hardest not to? I could definitely be the first person at Roosevelt Middle School to fail because I can't improvise. I like planning, knowing what to expect. But in drama, you're supposed to improvise and live in the moment. I don't see the point. I thought the whole point was that in drama you put on a play, which means following a script. Shakespeare didn't get famous because he was good at improvising.

Mrs. Alamantia was making us play a game where she

handed us an object, and we had to see how many things we could make up about it. Pretend, like we're little kids. My partner, Isabel Zhang, and I had been given an orange pool noodle.

Isabel pretended to write with it, struggling with how large it was. "Mom did say I was never gonna lose this pencil." She sighed. The whole class burst out laughing. Isabel is one of those people who can do anything—get good grades, look perfect, be funny. Isabel handed me the noodle and gestured for me to go.

I looked at the pool noodle and tried to be creative, although having to be creative under pressure is pretty terrible. If I'd had time to plan, I would have made a list of things it could be. The silence in the classroom seemed to stretch out for hours. "Just do something!" hissed Isabel. I did the first thing that came to me. I pretended to take a big bite. "So this is the big spaghetti, huh?"

I got a couple of claps, mostly from the really nice people in the class who will clap for anything. It wasn't imaginative, though. *It's literally called a noodle, Chloe,* announced the little voice in my head. I handed the noodle back to Isabel and hoped that the exercise would be over soon.

Isabel put the noodle straight up on her head. "I said I need a haircut! Just the one hair!" she shouted, pretending to be an irritated customer. The whole class, including Mrs. Alamantia, laughed even louder than before. Isabel pretended to look around at the class, the noodle quivering upright with indignation. "What's so funny about wanting a haircut?"

Isabel gave the noodle back to me, her face flushed with happiness. Mrs. Alamantia said that improvisation is about being in the moment, about responding, rather than trying to create a planned moment. My problem was that I liked planning. Organizing and neatly ordering activities and things was how I relaxed.

I took a deep breath and tried to let my mind go blank. *Just respond.* The whole class seemed to lean forward and watch. I held the noodle up to my nose.

"I'm an elephant," I said, swaying the noodle back and forth. "Honk, honk, honk."

"Elephants don't go honk, honk, honk," said someone in the class. I was looking at the ground, so I couldn't see who was talking.

"You can't say that to Chloe," someone whispered. "Be nice."

Ugh—I hated being *that* kid, the one other kids felt sorry for. I looked for a way to recover. "I'm a rare honking elephant," I said. "*Honkus elephantus.*"

"No criticism in the improvisation space," said Mrs. Alamantia. "We are trying to let one another flourish." Then she said that we were done, making me a very relieved elephant.

Improvisation exercises aside, I did like drama, mostly because of Mrs. Alamantia. She acted like she would rather be with us than do anything else in the world. Sometimes, she clapped her hands together and said, "Let me tell you something!" and then dropped some tidbit like trivia about a famous actor or something that happened during a performance.

Today, Mrs. Alamantia clapped her hands and said, "Class! This is so exciting! You have an opportunity to go on a field trip to see not one but two Broadway musicals! The drama department and the music department have worked together to organize this trip so you can see the many amazing professionals who make up the Broadway scene. We'll see one matinee and then one evening show."

All my terrible feelings about improv melted away. I *love* musicals. It started with the movies, like *The Little Mermaid* and *The Lion King*. Then I saw a high school production of *Annie*, which is about an orphan during the Depression, with its showstopper number "Tomorrow." Then Mom took me to see *Come from Away* for my birthday a few years ago. Lately I've been watching the oldie movie musicals: *West Side Story*, *My Fair Lady*, and *Oliver!* I love the way the songs make you feel, like you share all the emotions with the characters.

Based on the noises around me, everyone else was pretty excited, too. Isabel and her group of friends put their heads together, and I could hear snippets of their conversation. It sounded like they were already planning what to wear.

"I'm not going," said a voice. "Those Broadway shows are so fake." I turned to see who was talking. It was a boy in a blue hoodie. I didn't know the boys in the class as well as the girls, but I thought his name was Harry.

"You don't have to go, Henry," said Mrs. Alamantia calmly. Ah, right. Henry. I was pretty close. Henry, in spite of his outrageous comment, smiled and shrugged. "In fact," said Mrs. A, "this is probably a good time to mention that not everyone will be going. There are a limited number of spaces, and there is, of course, the expense of the tickets, the bus, and any extras."

"How much is the trip?" someone asked.

"It's actually a really good deal for getting to see two Broadway shows," said Mrs. Alamantia. "It's three hundred and seventy-five dollars for two shows, meals, and transportation. We're going up and back in one day, to save on the expense of a hotel."

The rest of the class started chatting again. For a lot of kids, this was nothing. I lived in a pretty wealthy area outside of Washington, DC. Most parents would send in the money and think nothing of it.

Henry hooted. "I can think of *so many* things I'd rather do with that money! Musicals are so phony! Like, who gets up and just starts dancing with a group of people?"

I tended to ignore the boys in my class. They're kind of annoying, and giving them any kind of attention just made them misbehave more. But that kind of talk about musicals was not something I was going to stand for.

"You're right," I said. "So fake, unlike, I don't know—video games? Berets for cats? Flamin' Hot Cheetos?"

"Oh, come on," said Henry. "You're not going to go after the Cheetos!" He pretended to grab his hair in shock. Henry had thick black hair that he wore short on the sides and longer on top.

"Why not? They're fake."

"They're good fake," said Henry.

"If your point is that something is bad because it's fake, then all things that are fake should be bad," I said. *Yeah, take that, Henry Broadway-Hater!* agreed the little voice in my head.

Henry put his hands up. "Whoa, I didn't realize this was a debate class, Chloe!"

I shouldn't have been surprised that he knew my name—most kids had heard of me at school, for all the wrong reasons. Still, it was weird to hear him say my name out loud.

"Stick to things you know about," I said. "Flamin' Hot Cheetos, not musicals."

Henry looked at me and nodded. Then he drew his fingers across his lips, zippering them shut, like we were in cahoots, which we definitely were *not*.

Home Is Where the Robots Are

As soon as I walked through the front door, I heard Dad.

Specifically, I heard Dad yell, "DUCK!"

I dropped my backpack and squatted, just in time to feel the breeze of something flying over my head, accompanied by a mechanical whir. I looked up. A drone hovered over me for a second and then flew back down the hall.

"What was that?" I said while taking off my shoes.

"I had this idea," said Dad. Then he stopped talking. My

dad does that sometimes, especially when he gets caught up in something.

"And that idea was . . ." I said, hoping he'd pick up the rest of the sentence. I walked into the living room and found Dad fiddling with a controller.

"That a drone could help find my phone," said Dad.

"That would be nice," I said. My dad was kind of a technical genius, but that did not extend to normal life stuff. He spends about a third of his life looking for his phone, keys, or wallet. My dad used to develop medical devices. He'd travel all over the country and demonstrate medical equipment to hospitals and doctor's offices. But after my mom died, he decided he needed to be home with me, so he's been working on different inventions instead, hoping that he can get someone to invest in them.

"It's like a Roomba," he said as if that made perfect sense.

"Dad, a Roomba does not fly or find things," I said. "It sucks things up. It's practically the opposite of what you're doing."

"Ah! But a Roomba does know how to find its way around a house. It has to, to make sure it cleans all the surfaces. *That's* how it's like a Roomba," said Dad triumphantly. "I'm teaching the drone how to look around the house."

"Ohhh. I guess that makes sense," I admitted. "How's it going?"

"We've had some false positives," said Dad. "A lot of things look like a phone to the drone right now. And it needs to charge."

"Well, we can start prepping dinner while that happens," I said. "It's Thursday."

"Is it? Already?" said Dad. "Okay. I just need a minute. I, uh, oh dear." Dad looked around the living room for a moment, his hand on his cheek.

"What is it?"

Dad let out a long noisy sigh. "Well, I hid the phone so the drone could work on finding it."

"And?"

"Now I don't remember where I put it," said Dad. "I

thought I had put it on the side table, next to the chair."
Dad didn't have to say which chair it was. He meant the oversized, dark brown chair that had been Mom's favorite place to sit and read.

"You look for the phone," I said. "I'll start cutting up the chicken."

On Thursdays, we make Three Cup Chicken, which was one of the dishes my mom used to make. It gets its name from the story that it takes one cup each of soy sauce, rice wine, and sesame oil, though if you actually make it like that, it probably would not be good. Mom never wrote down how she made it, so Dad and I keep experimenting to see if we can make it like hers. So far, we have made it eighty-three different ways.

My mom was an emergency room doctor—she died from COVID during the pandemic. It was in the really bad days in the beginning, when there were shortages of protective equipment like masks and gowns for the medical personnel. Mom tried to be careful. When they ran low on masks, she kept hers in a paper bag with her name on it so they could keep sterilizing it. She didn't bring any clothes she wore at the hospital into the house. She stayed in the guest room, and I wasn't allowed to touch her, just talk to her from the hallway. Six feet away.

Even though she was cautious, she still got sick. Now it's just me and Dad. For a long time, it felt like we were trying to live with a big hole in the middle of the floor, a hole of grief and confusion that we could fall into at any moment. Now it feels like we have more good days than bad days, though we still have to be careful. The traditions we have, like Three Cup Chicken on Thursdays, seem to help keep us steady. We have a notebook where we write down what we've tried, like scientists.

"So, this week we decided we were going to try Thai basil leaves to see if they had a better flavor," said Dad, reading over our notes as we ate dinner.

"I think the basil tastes more like Mom's," I said. "But her sauce was thicker, wasn't it?"

"It was," agreed Dad.

"We cooked it for fifteen minutes," I said.

"But maybe we need to pay attention to the heat," said Dad. "Maybe it was too low and the sauce couldn't thicken properly."

There was another way we could find out about the recipe. We could ask Auntie Sue, my mom's older sister. I could call her yí mā, which would be the proper Chinese name, but "Auntie Sue" kind of stuck when I was little.

When my mom was alive, Auntie Sue would come over and we would talk for hours while we made dumplings or had hot pot. I remember so much laughing and teasing; Auntie Sue and Mom would remember being kids and getting into trouble. But Auntie Sue and Dad haven't gotten along since Mom died.

I supposed I could ask Auntie Sue myself about Three Cup Chicken, but then that felt disloyal to Dad. Dad and I were figuring this out together, and asking Auntie Sue for help if Dad wouldn't ask her would be cheating in a way. I loved

Auntie Sue—but it seemed I couldn't love Auntie Sue and Dad together.

So, for the eighty-fourth time, I said, "We can make that a note for next time."

Dad made a note. "Still, this is pretty darn good sān bēi jī," he said, using the Chinese word for it. He made a little poem, riffing on the word *three*. "Sān yuè, sān yī hǎo, sān bēi jī, gèng shì hǎo."

Third month, thirty-first day, Three Cup Chicken is even better.

I checked the calendar. It was, in fact, March 31. "Have you paid the bills?" Bills were due at the end of the month.

"It's on my list of things to do tonight," said Dad calmly, spooning some more chicken into my bowl. "And it's not something you need to worry about. You're just a kid."

"Dad, you didn't know it was Thursday. And remember the time you forgot to pay the electric bill and we got a notice?"

"But I did know the date. Everyone makes mistakes, Chloe. That's just a fact of life," said Dad.

"I prefer mistakes that don't make the Wi-Fi go out!" I said, joking.

"The Wi-Fi never went out," said Dad. "And even if it did, we'd be okay. I'd just go pay the bill and it would come back on. Now, you worry about kid things." The problem was that when someone said things like *Don't worry about it*, I actually ended up worrying more. Like maybe the truth was worse. Or maybe I'd be surprised by something bad because I didn't worry enough.

"Is there anything going on at school I should know about?" asked Dad. "Any tests? Projects you need help with?"

I thought about the Broadway show, the $375. Dad's inventions cost money. The drone, for instance.

"Do we have enough money to pay the bills?" I asked.

"Chloe!" said Dad. "What kind of question is that?"

I noticed that Dad didn't answer my question. "Well, do we?"

"You're *twelve*," said Dad. "Stop worrying about bills and

money. Tell me about school. Is anything happening?"

A grim pit settled into my stomach. We didn't have enough money, and Dad wasn't going to tell me. "No," I said. "Nothing big." I didn't need to go to Broadway, I told myself.

You! Again!

On Friday, Sabrina said we should walk over to the shopping center and check out a new tea place she'd heard about. We were standing by our lockers, trying not to get swept away by the intense energy of a Friday afternoon in middle school.

"Tea?" I said. My parents had taken me to a tea shop once, when I was little, in Chinatown in New York. It was in the basement of a Chinese grocery store. It didn't seem that exciting to me, but then again, I was a lot shorter back then and could barely see over the counter crowded with jars and canisters and boxes.

"Yeah," said Sabrina. She nudged me. "You're Chinese. Didn't you guys, like, invent tea?" Five years of friendship allowed her to make jokes like that.

"The Chinese also invented the toothbrush. Are we going to a toothbrush shop, too?" I asked. I sent my dad a quick text to make sure it was okay to go. Dad texted back, *Have fun! Don't hurry home!*

"That's next week," joked Sabrina. Suddenly, she shot her hand into the air and waved at someone, dropping a bunch of papers on the ground. "Topher, what'd you think of that science test?"

"Did you get the bonus question?" asked Topher.

"Nah," said Sabrina. She didn't seem worried about her papers. She was too busy looking at Topher. I knelt down and began picking up the papers, automatically arranging them by date, most recent on top. Sabrina had some papers from two months ago mixed in with a worksheet from today—what was she thinking?

"Me neither," said Topher. "It was like it was in code. Oh, hey, Chloe. I didn't see you down there."

Sabrina giggled. *A little too hard*, I thought. "Martian code," she said. They were still standing over me while I tried to keep Sabrina's papers from getting stepped on.

"Definitely," said Topher. "Well, see ya." I stood up and handed Sabrina her science homework, now in chronological order.

"These papers should be in your notebook, not loose," I scolded her. "That's how you lose stuff."

"I know," said Sabrina good-naturedly. She stuck the papers in her backpack without looking. She was too busy staring at Topher walking away.

"Whoa," I said. "Do you like him?"

"He's in my science class," said Sabrina. She was, like my dad, not answering my question. "He also plays soccer. He's the goalie."

"You know what I mean. Do you *like* like this soccer-playing dude?" My voice rose. Some of the kids in our grade had started acting weird around certain people. Giggling and staring. Leaving notes in lockers. Some of the kids in the grade ahead of us held hands as they walked to class.

"Topher is really nice," said Sabrina. "He let me borrow a pencil today when I couldn't find one." Sabrina made it sound like Topher had given her a kidney.

"*I'm* really nice," I said. "I just picked up all your science homework!"

Sabrina shut her locker door and looped her arm through mine. "You are really nice," she agreed. "You're the best. And you're the one I'm taking to see the tea place!"

•°• 🥤 •°•

"Ohhhhh," I said as we stepped into the store. "It's a *boba* tea shop!" And it was a really pretty one, too. The whole store was set up to feel like you had stepped into some kind of magical garden at dusk, when the fireflies came out. The walls were painted a deep blue, making it seem like they stretched out into the sky, but the dark walls still had a snug feeling. Lines of fairy lights crisscrossed the store. I could hear the gentle trickle of a fountain, and then I noticed there was even a bridge with a stream of water under it.

"Have you been to one before?" asked Sabrina.

"My cousins took me for boba tea in Los Angeles," I said. "A couple of years ago." Jeremy and Clark had ordered a mango slush for me, and then I watched them play basketball at a park. I remembered chewing on the soft, sticky boba, trying to make them last through the whole afternoon of basketball.

"So, what do we do?" Sabrina was now staring up at the menu board.

"You like strawberries," I said. "Get strawberry."

"Strawberry *what*, though," said Sabrina. "Milk tea? Fruit tea? A slush?" Her head swiveled as she scanned the board. "I can also get strawberry-flavored popping boba, whatever that is."

The girl in front of us turned around. "The popping boba

is so good!" she said. "You bite down and the juice squirts out." This happened to Sabrina a lot. People just started ·talking to her.

"Oh! So, what are you getting?" asked Sabrina.

"Guava green tea with coconut agar," said the girl. She pointed to the boy next to her. "He's getting Thai iced tea with brown sugar boba."

"I didn't say what I was ordering!" protested the boy.

"That's what you were going to order," said the girl, swinging her ponytail so it brushed against the boy's arm. They were probably boyfriend and girlfriend. The line moved up.

"I think they are doing advanced-level ordering," said Sabrina in a low voice. "I don't even see what they're talking about on the menu!"

I was too busy studying the prices on the menu. Most of the drinks were four or five dollars, some were even more. I had exactly $3.37 in my backpack.

"Oh gosh," I said. "I just remembered I left my money at

home. I mean, I have some, but not enough." I had seventeen dollars in a shoebox.

Sabrina waved her hand. "I can get it. You can pay me back." Sabrina's mom and dad owned a chain of taquerías in town, Taco Asombroso; they were super popular. Sabrina always had enough money.

"No, it's fine," I said. I spotted a case with sodas, marked two dollars each. It was more than I'd pay for a drink from a machine, but less than the other drinks. I grabbed a Coke. "I'll get this."

"You can't get soda when you go to a boba shop," protested Sabrina. "It's practically an insult."

"It sure is," said a voice that sounded vaguely familiar. We had come to the front of the line. I turned and looked.

"You!"

It was Henry, Mr. I-Hate-Broadway. Except instead of a blue hoodie, he was now wearing a dark green T-shirt that said TEA PALACE and a name tag that said HENRY THE BOBA MASTER.

"Hey, it's Miss Don't-Hate-Broadway," said Henry.

Whoa, said my little voice. *Did you say the quiet part out loud? How did he know to call you the exact opposite of what you called him?* I paused a second, wondering if I had done something stupid, but then Henry acted like everything was normal. "What can I get for you?" asked Henry.

I had been thinking that maybe Sabrina was right and I should take her up on her offer to pay, but I was definitely not going to say any of that in front of *him*. "I'll get this." I pushed the can of Coke toward him with one hand and dug out the money from my backpack with the other.

Henry sighed and shook his head. "Come on, get something from the menu. We have excellent drinks." He gestured toward the board. "What do you like? Something fruity? Or maybe something more unique? Like taro?" Henry had a dimple when he smiled. He probably thought he looked charming when he smiled like that.

"Oh, boba. A fake drink," I shot back.

"So is Coke," responded Henry. "All drinks except water are kind of fake if you think about it."

"Which will be fine." I was wavering, though. Someone took away a tray of four drinks, as colorful as a flower garden.

Sabrina waved awkwardly, and I remembered my manners. "This is Sabrina, by the way." Henry waved. "Sabrina, this is Henry. He hates Broadway." Sabrina laughed.

"The institution, not her," said Henry quickly.

"We'll have to talk about that another time," said Sabrina. "Because you're oh-so-wrong." Sabrina was definitely going on the Broadway trip. She had played Mama Ogre in the school musical of *Shrek* last year. She put her arm around my shoulders. "We are going, and it will be amazing." I hadn't told Sabrina that I couldn't afford the trip, which I was not going to announce in front of Henry. How dumb would I look, defending musicals and then not actually going on the trip? Instead, I tried to smile and look confident. "Yup," I squeaked. "Broadway, here we come."

Sabrina saved me from further awkwardness by placing her order. "I'll have the passion fruit milk tea with white boba," said Sabrina, as if she had been ordering boba teas her whole life.

Henry cheered. "That's how you do it!" He rang up her order. "You should be more like Sabrina," he said to me.

"What happened to the customer is always right?" I asked.

Henry rolled his eyes. "The person who came up with that saying never worked in the food service industry."

"That's for sure," chimed in Sabrina. "My parents own a restaurant," she added.

"Her parents own Taco Asombroso," I said, bragging for Sabrina.

"Oh man, I love those tacos!" said Henry. Because everyone did. "The chorizo one? With the lime cilantro crema?" He made a little chef's kiss. "Amazing."

Sabrina pretended to curtsy. "Thank you," she said.

"So, are you going to get something proper, now that Sabrina has shown you the right way?" asked Henry. "Or do you need to finish . . . that?"

I looked down. While we had all been talking, I had been arranging the straws by color—blue, pink, green, yellow. I hadn't even meant to. It was just something I did without thinking. I jerked my hands away from the box of straws. Only three straws were out of place while the rest were neatly arranged in rows by color. I really wanted to fix the last three, but I restrained myself.

I thrust the money for the soda at Henry. He took my money but slumped his shoulders and sighed as he put the bills away in the register. "You disappoint me, Broadway." Sabrina laughed, though I didn't know why. Henry was not that funny!

•᛫• 🥤 •᛫•

Sabrina and I snagged a table near the center of the restaurant, surrounded by pots of leafy bamboo. Sabrina took a long sip of her drink and sighed contentedly.

"Oh man, it's so good," she said. "Here, you want to try it?" She tipped the cup toward me. I took a sip, inhaling the perfumy orange drink and a couple of boba.

"You should have gotten a boba tea," said Sabrina. "I had enough money for both of us."

"It's fine," I said. "I'll get one another time."

"Yeah, we're definitely coming back here," said Sabrina. "We should make this a regular thing."

"Speaking of something that should be done regularly, you need to organize your science homework." I pointed to her backpack. "It's a mess."

Sabrina gave her backpack a kick. "I'm a little afraid of what's in there."

"But isn't it better when you know all your stuff is in order? Like you can find all your tests to study from? And you can review your homework because it's all in one place?" I didn't say what I was actually thinking, which was that organizing stuff was fun—for me. It was like putting a puzzle together, and then I always felt better when I was done.

"I think you're making a *pret*-ty huge assumption here," said Sabrina. She took a long sip of her drink. "I mean, I used to be able to just know all the stuff they were teaching us, though lately it's been harder."

"So, take a few minutes and keep it all straight," I said. "It's easy. I'll show you."

"Wouldn't you rather talk about something fun? Like the weekend?" said Sabrina.

"After we organize your notebook," I said, holding out my hand. Sabrina handed me her battered blue science notebook, which looked like it had been trying to eat and then spit out a stack of papers. "We're going to make three different piles—one for tests, one for notes, and one for homework." We got to work, making the stacks. I tried not to look at her grades, but I couldn't help noticing that Sabrina had started out with As, and then her grades had begun falling steadily. Her latest test was a C-plus.

"Some of those questions were out of nowhere," said Sabrina, blushing. "Like, we spent all this time on plants and animals, but then I was supposed to know those four other kingdoms, like the germs?"

"Let's rearrange the stacks in reverse order, so the most recent stuff is on top," I said, ignoring her comment. We shuffled the papers into order. "Now we'll put them back in your notebook and use these dividers that you've been ignoring, to keep them straight."

"A bunch of these don't have holes in them," complained Sabrina.

"Luckily, I have this portable three-hole punch," I said, pulling one out of my backpack. "It doesn't work on more than a couple of papers at a time, so I do it as soon as I get the papers."

Sabrina pretended to cough. *"Nerd."* But she took the hole puncher and got to work.

"Now, when you get stuff back, just put it in the right section, and it automatically stays organized," I said.

"Shoot," said Sabrina, holding up a homework assignment. "She did put the things about the four other kingdoms on here. Bacteria, archaebacteria, fungi, and protozoa. It was on the definitions homework." She clicked the notebook rings shut. "There might be something to this organizing thing after all."

"I mean, I think it's kind of beautiful," I said softly. "Having everything neat and tidy."

"You're weird, but I love you," said Sabrina. She stuck her notebook back into her backpack. "Now can we talk about something fun?"

When Sabrina said *fun*, Henry's face popped in between two bamboo plants. I nearly screamed.

"What's fun?" asked Henry.

"Chloe was org—" Sabrina started, but I kicked her under the table. "Nothing," I said. "Nothing is fun. We are not having any fun here." Henry would probably tease me for being an organizing geek. He'd already seen me with the straws.

"Aw, too bad," said Henry. "It's probably because you didn't order any boba." Sabrina laughed. "But here, I made too much of this taro milk tea for someone, so I thought you might like it." Henry set down a small cup with creamy purple liquid in front of me.

I was too surprised to say anything. Then Sabrina said, "That's so nice, isn't it, Chloe?" in a very loud voice.

"Um, yeah. I guess. You didn't have to do that," I said.

"She means *thank you*," said Sabrina sarcastically. I mumbled a thank-you.

"You're welcome," said Henry.

"What is taro anyway?" asked Sabrina.

"It's a vegetable," explained Henry. "Sort of like a potato, but not. And it's purple and kind of sweet." Someone called his name, and he disappeared back through the leaves.

"What's wrong with you?" Sabrina whispered fiercely. "Someone does something nice for you, and you act like he gave you a warm cup of poison."

I couldn't explain how I was feeling, exactly. When I saw Henry pop through the leaves, I felt confused. First he startled me, but then I felt kind of excited to see him, even though he had been sort of a jerk about Broadway. Why would I be excited to see Henry? And why had I been so rude if I felt excited?

I took a sip of the taro milk tea. "Ugh," I said. "It's fine."

Excuse me, said my little voice. *This is more than fine. It tastes amazing. It feels like home. YUM. Drink all of it, now!*

"I can tell from the way you're slurping that down that it's more than fine," said Sabrina. This was the curse of having a friend who knows you so well. "You like it! And this is how you're supposed to act when you like something." She took a sip of her drink and then said, "Oooh! Delicious!" in a loud voice, while making her face seem extra excited. "See?"

We both burst out laughing. But then a man wearing a Tea Palace apron came over, frowning. "You girls, this is a quiet place. Not a loud place," he said grumpily. "Lots of people come here to study." His eyebrows made an angry black V. He gestured around the room. People were hunched over books and laptops with their drinks. A sign on one wall read THANK YOU FOR KEEPING TEA PALACE A PEACEFUL PLACE FOR THOUGHT AND STUDY.

Henry came by again, sweeping dirt into a pan. "Sorry," he whispered. "My uncle is kind of a grouch."

Looking at Henry in his Tea Palace T-shirt, suddenly it hit me. I couldn't ask Dad for money to Broadway, but maybe I could earn the money myself.

"Henry," I said. "How did you get a job here?"

"Why, you want to work here?" quipped Henry. "I think you'd have to try the boba first."

I ignored the dig. "I'm just curious," I said. "I thought you couldn't get a job until you were, like, sixteen."

"My parents own Tea Palace, and my uncle is the manager. Family business uses family members. Uses, not pays, I might add, in my situation. Unless you count the free drink every shift," said Henry.

"I could have told you that," said Sabrina. "Except my parents don't want me to work in a restaurant, so they won't let me."

So maybe my dad didn't have a restaurant, but that got me thinking. Maybe I could pay my own way to Broadway!

Phineas

"Do NOT let the robot escape!" Dad yelled when I came home. I quickly shut the door, just in time to see a small blue object run over my foot and bump into the door.

"Should I send it back to you?" I called while I took off my shoes. Now the robot was trying to drive up my leg. But maybe that was what the robot was supposed to do.

"I've got it," said Dad. "Come, K-99." The robot rolled off my leg, spun around, and headed back toward the living room. Dad's playlist was booming through the speakers, which meant his ideas were working. He played James Taylor and Neil Diamond and Carly Simon, old folky music, when he was in a good mood.

"What's this one supposed to do?" I asked, following the robot.

"Guess!" said Dad. He was holding a controller in one hand. He held out the other hand to give me a welcome-home-from-school hug.

"Ummm . . ." I looked at the robot and looked for clues. "It looks kind of like a dog." There was definitely a head and tail. "Is it a toy for people who want a dog but can't have one? Because of allergies?"

"Oooh, I like that you thought of dogs right away," said Dad.

"A guard dog?" I guessed again. "Part of a security system?"

"Hmm . . ." Dad took out a notebook and wrote in it. "I hadn't thought of that, but it could definitely be a feature."

"So, what is it?" I asked.

"It's a robot dog trainer!'" said Dad. "I read about how all these dogs were adopted during the pandemic, and now they need obedience training. K-99 teaches dogs through example and positive reinforcement." He pushed a button and the robot chirped "Here!" and then belched out a piece of kibble.

"What happened to the phone-finding drone?" I asked.

"A good inventor keeps multiple irons in the fire," said Dad. "So, what do you think? Pretty cool, huh?"

I didn't think a robot dog was a good idea. That would be like a robot teacher, which I definitely did not like the idea of. But I didn't want to hurt Dad's feelings, so I thought of something else instead.

"It seems like a good project," I said finally. "But you really need a dog to work with." That was a good out. We didn't have a dog, or any pets at all.

"That's the best part," said Dad. "Ta-da!" Dad stepped to one side and waved his arms. There, sitting in Mom's chair, was a very large, very furry brown dog. "Meet Phineas!"

"Dad," I said after I had recovered from shock. "No. No, no, no." *What was Dad thinking?*

"You like dogs!" protested Dad.

"I do! I like dogs, as in *other people's dogs in other people's houses.*"

"Aw, come on. Look at that face! He's great," said Dad. He knelt down and gave Phineas a couple of strokes. Phineas leaned into Dad and made the dog version of a smiley face, which meant that his mouth opened and a long pink tongue rolled out.

I know that in most families the kids would beg for a dog and the parents would say no. But my dad and I aren't like other families. And a dog would make the house different. Different from when my mom was here. But I couldn't say that to Dad.

"What about when it rains? He'll have to be walked in the rain and then dried off, and he probably smells, because, you know, wet dog," I said, trying to think of an argument that might make sense to Dad.

"Dogs cost money," I said. "I can only imagine how much this dog eats."

"I told you not to worry about money," said Dad. Which was different from saying there is nothing to worry about.

Another image popped into my head. A terrible one. "Is Phineas housebroken?"

"It's one of the many functions of K-99, the canine trainer," said Dad. He set Phineas on the ground and pressed a button on a remote.

"Would you like to go outside?" K-99 droned to Phineas. Phineas cocked his head to one side, lowered himself to the same level as K-99, and whined.

"Can the robot actually let dogs outside?" I asked. "It seems kind of mean to ask if the dog wants to go outside and not have a way to do it." Now Phineas had gotten up again and was starting to pace back and forth.

"Um, no," said Dad. "That's another good idea." I sighed. Why was Dad doing this? Phineas looked at me hopefully.

I looked back at Mom's chair. It was already covered in dog fur.

"What if we consider this to be a trial period?" I said. "Like, maybe we need to consider that Phineas won't like it here, either."

"This can be a time when we all think about whether this is a good match," said Dad. "But I think you're going to come to love this guy."

When Dad said we could just think about Phineas, I stopped feeling nervous and gave Phineas a closer look. He really was a big dog, coming up past my waist, with light brown fur. His bright black eyes twinkled at me. "How did you get him?" I asked.

"It's more like he picked me," said Dad. "Phineas came running over to me while I was filling up the car, and the guy said he was on his way to take him to the pound. It was like Phineas was asking me for help."

I scratched Phineas behind the ears, and he let out a long

sigh of contentment. Now I was wondering if this was the only way Dad could get a dog—a free one from the gas station. Maybe Dad had been wanting a dog for a long time, but we couldn't afford one.

A new song came on—sweet horns with a soft sweep of drums. "Sweet Caroline" by Neil Diamond. I blinked hard. My mom's name was Caroline. *Do not cry in front of Dad.* I wondered if Dad had meant to keep that song on his playlist.

Dad held out his arms so I would dance with him. This was something that I thought was really cool when I was little, dancing with Dad. "Do you remember we pretended that everyone at the baseball stadium was singing this to Mom when we went to Boston?" Dad asked. Phineas tried to get between us, like he was part of the dance.

"Sure," I said. It had been a little scary for me because there were so many people, but Mom and Dad were excited, so I tried to be excited, too.

"It started raining in the fifth inning," he said.

"At least Mom had that rain poncho in her purse," I said. Mom always seemed to have exactly what we needed in her purse—a snack, a Band-Aid, a pen.

"By some miracle, it kept us all dry," said Dad. "Your mom . . ." His voice trailed off. I think we were both filling in the end of that sentence. *Was amazing. Worked miracles. Is missed.*

Is not here.

We were starting to go down a rabbit hole, the rabbit hole of feeling sad. I had to stop it. I looked down at the floor. "For a dog who hasn't been here that long, there's an awful lot of dog hair already." I let go of Dad. "Look at my pants." I was wearing my favorite light blue jeans, which were now dotted with brown fur.

"Look at you!" I said to Phineas. "You messy boy." Phineas stretched and shook his head, his ears flapping.

Phineas watched us clean up. I got out the lint roller and took care of my jeans. Then Dad swept the room, and I used my handheld vacuum cleaner on the sofa. The weather was turning warmer, and Phineas was clearly the type of dog who shed. A lot.

"Auntie Sue got you that little vacuum," said Dad, smiling a little. "You wanted that instead of games or toys."

I nodded, holding my breath. Dad never talked about Auntie Sue if he could help it.

"She called the other day," said Dad. "She wants to see you."

"Just me, huh," I said cautiously. I tried to read his tone, checking to see if he was angry or worried. I still didn't know what to think. Auntie Sue said Dad should have done more to protect Mom, like make her quit her job. But Mom wanted to help people, especially people who were sick. She said this was why she became a doctor in the first place.

Dad knew I was worried. "It's okay that she wants to see just you," said Dad. "I'm the adult. I can deal." Phineas pushed at my dad's hand and whined.

I sucked up a tuft of fur floating in the air with my

vacuum. I loved Auntie Sue, but I didn't like the way she criticized my dad and made him feel bad. I didn't like feeling all twisted up when she came around.

"I'll think about it," I said. The house was getting back into order. I ran the vacuum over the sofa, sucking up the last few stray hairs. Then Phineas lowered his bottom and began to curve his back. I knew what that meant. I'd seen other dogs do it.

"Get him out of here!" I screamed. "He's getting ready to poop!"

"What?" asked Dad. He was looking at his phone.

A smelly brown trail dropped onto the floor. "Aaaagh!" I screamed. "He's pooping! Actually pooping in the house!!"

"No," droned the robot. "Please poop outside. Let's go outside. Good dogs poop outside."

"Hey!" said Dad. "The poop indicator worked!" He opened the door to the backyard; Phineas sprinted outside, and Dad followed him, leaving me with the mess.

"I don't think I should have to clean up after a dog I didn't ask for!" I yelled through the open door.

Sabrina was completely unsympathetic about Phineas when I complained about him at school. "I can't believe you're complaining about your dad getting you a dog," said Sabrina. "You're so weird."

"I like dogs," I said for what felt like the thousandth time. "It's just that dogs are a lot of work. I could practically make a new mattress out of all the fur Phineas sheds." I wondered if Sabrina would buy my excuse. If anyone could see through me, it would be Sabrina.

"You sound like my mom," said Sabrina. "Quit worrying about the work, and focus on the fun. What's wrong with you? And speaking of fun, are you going to remember to bring the check for the trip *tomorrow*?"

The problem with being a person known for being super organized is that your friends give you a hard time when you forget anything.

"I forgot . . . because of the dog," I said. Which was completely untrue.

"My music teacher says she already has a ton of people going," said Sabrina. "You might miss out on the trip completely if you don't bring in the money right away."

"Mm-hmm," I said, not knowing what exactly to wish for. Part of me just wanted to tell Sabrina the truth, that my dad didn't have the money, but I was afraid that would make things weird between us. I didn't want to be anyone's charity case, not even Sabrina's, and she was my best friend.

But Sabrina also had really good ideas. If I told her I needed to make money, she'd probably come up with an amazing idea of how to get some.

Suddenly, everything clicked. I had a way to be kind of honest. "My dad . . . um, said that I have to earn the money for the trip, that he isn't going to just give it to me."

Sabrina's eyes widened. "That's so unfair! Why is your dad being so mean?"

Oh no—I didn't mean for Sabrina to get mad at Dad! "It's not like that," I said. "He thinks that I'll appreciate it more if I earn my own way." I crossed my fingers and silently apologized to Dad. "He's just trying to be a good parent. He says lots of kids around here don't know the value of a dollar." Dad did actually say that, so that wasn't a lie.

Sabrina nodded. "My parents say that, too. They said that the trip counts as my birthday present."

"Exactly," I said. "You get it."

"So you know what you have to do, right?" asked Sabrina.

"What?"

"You have to get a job!" said Sabrina. My idea worked!

"You know the deal," I said. "My dad does not own a restaurant."

"Oh, you know what job I mean," said Sabrina. She waited a beat as if I didn't know what was coming. "Babysitting."

Ugh. My idea did not work! It was a well-known fact that I was vaguely terrified of children, being around them, talking to them. Trying to figure out what they wanted. Sabrina babysat all the time for her little brother, Oscar.

"Diapers, runny noses, just general messiness. Germs. Crying. Snot," I said, reeling off the first things I thought of when I thought of babysitting. "Besides, most parents want experienced babysitters, and I have zero experience."

"Look, you can start with something easy, like older kids who can take themselves to the bathroom. And get an afternoon gig so you don't have to worry about stuff like bedtime and baths." Sabrina twirled her long brown hair up into a bun while she talked, which made her look older for a second. Then the bun spilled back out over her shoulders.

"And how are parents going to know all this?" I asked.

"Do I have to explain everything? You tell your dad to tell his friends and your neighbors, and I'll tell my parents to do the same thing. And if the parents like you, they'll hire you back. And then you'll have the money in no time." Sabrina snapped her fingers.

Everything Sabrina said made perfect sense. And yet.

"Little kids are so . . . sticky," I said.

"Oh, just make 'em wash their hands, and if you go outside, take a pack of wipes. I *know* you have some in your backpack," said Sabrina.

"They're quite handy in the right situation," I said sniffily as Sabrina laughed at me.

5

Going, Going . . .

"And . . . go! Taylor!"

Mrs. Alamantia tossed a pale pink teddy bear into the middle of our group. We were supposed to work together and keep the bear moving, not let it fall to the ground, by catching it and then immediately tossing it to someone else and saying their name at the same time. Shouts and giggles erupted around me. Mrs. Alamantia had us stand apart, but now we were jostling and moving with the direction of the bear, like an amoeba.

"Remember, you want to throw the bear so that the other person can catch it," said Mrs. Alamantia. "This is not a game of coordination, not expediency." Ex-pe-di-en-cy. Mrs. Alamantia said every syllable crisply—she said that speaking clearly is part of being onstage, which was part volume and part diction.

I knew this wasn't about being orderly, but couldn't we be *quasi* orderly, like going in alphabetical order so that we had some idea of when our name was going to get called? Instead, I had to stay constantly on my toes for the possibility that someone would shout my name. I didn't want to be the one who dropped it. It was already bad enough that I was the World's Worst Person at Improv.

Mrs. Alamantia threw in a second stuffed animal. A red dragon with a yellow belly.

"Chloe!" Mrs. Alamantia has chosen me! I lunged for the dragon and managed to catch it by the tip of its tail. We were supposed to throw to someone who was not standing near us, so I picked Isabel, who was waving her hands. "Isabel!"

Isabel's face lit up, and she opened her arms to catch. Except that because I am not the most athletic or accurate person, I missed Isabel completely and hit someone else in the face.

Oops. And it wasn't just someone; it was Henry.

Way to go, Chloe. You missed your target and hit the most annoying boy in the class. Sometimes I wanted to punch the little voice in my head in the face. Which probably meant I wanted to punch myself in the face.

"That alternative ending to *The Hobbit* still needs some work," said Henry, picking up the dragon.

The whole class went silent and then burst out laughing. I felt my face turn redder than the dragon I just threw. I'd messed up the game. I wasn't even sure what was supposed to happen next. Luckily, Mrs. Alamantia saved me.

"Throw the dragon back in, but tell us something about the dragon," she instructed. "The person who catches the dragon has to build on what you just said. What kind of a job does a dragon want?"

"The dragon wants to work in construction!" said Henry.

"Working as a welder!" He tossed the dragon in, and immediately, the group was energized again, forgetting about me. Maybe Mrs. Alamantia was right. It was okay to make mistakes. Maybe it wasn't even a mistake. It was just trying. I could do this!

Carson Boyers caught the dragon. "He can't find a helmet that fits over his spikes!" He heaved it to Mira Krakowski.

"His best friend operates the steamroller!" Mira cried. She threw it to me.

When Mira said *steamroller*, the word *flat* immediately came to mind. Steamrollers rolled things flat, right? I could do this! Maybe I could do improv. "The dragon becomes flat-ulent!" I shouted.

And then, for the second time, I brought the class to a halt. And I was pretty sure Henry was laughing the hardest at me.

"I know what *flatulent* means," I moaned to Sabrina and Allie at lunch. "I was trying to say flat and my mouth just kept going. This is why I don't like doing things spontaneously."

"Oh, come on," said Allie. "It's funny." Allie is someone I hang out with occasionally. We would probably be closer, except Allie was really serious about soccer, so she's always busy after school and on weekends.

"It's a *gas*," teased Sabrina.

"I sounded like a *moron*," I said. I could still hear my class laughing in my head, particularly Henry. Even Mrs. A had giggled. "It's Henry's fault for pretending the dragon wanted to be a construction worker. That's how we got to steamroller, which led to . . . you know. Farts."

"Who's Henry?" asked Allie.

"He's someone in our grade. He works at Tea Palace," said Sabrina.

"He's someone irritating who works at Tea Palace," I amended. "And he's in my drama class."

"He gave you a free drink!" said Sabrina. "You can't complain about that."

"You really can't," agreed Allie. "That's super nice."

"I don't need his free drink," I said. "I need to make money for the trip."

"The one I want to see is *Legally Blonde*," said Sabrina.

"I like that one, too!" I said. "I mean, I liked the movie without the singing, so I'm assuming I'll like it with singing."

"So hurry up and get your money in!" said Allie. She drummed her fingers on the table.

"It's not that simple," Sabrina explained. "Chloe has to make her own money."

"Oooh," said Allie. "My mom was dying to go, so she's chaperoning." She got a funny look on her face. "Sorry."

"For what?"

"You know . . ." said Allie awkwardly. "The thing about my mom. That was insensitive."

I tried to act like it wasn't a big deal, but now I felt like I had to make Allie feel better. "Hey, are you ready for Mr. McRyan's notebook check?" I asked, changing the subject.

We both had Mr. McRyan for social studies. Mr. McRyan

was old and spoke with a southern drawl, and the joke was that he taught the Civil War from memory. What's not a joke was that Mr. McRyan was also a famously hard grader. His homework assignments were never the easy fill-in-the-blank-type assignments, and his tests made people cry. He also had notebook checks where you had to have everything perfectly in order. If you missed anything or had anything out of order, he would give you a failing grade.

I had heard that the highest grade Mr. McRyan had ever— ever—given out was a B-minus, and that was to someone who went on to Harvard and became a brain surgeon. I had written down the notebook check on my calendar and then marked it with pink highlighter. Pink highlighter meant *Pay attention!*

"I'm so nervous," I told Allie.

"You're nervous?!" exclaimed Allie. "If you're nervous, then the rest of us are really in trouble."

"I just don't want to fail," I said. My dad was always telling me that actually learning the material was more important than the grade, but still, I wasn't sure how he would feel about an actual failing grade.

"Oh, come on," said Sabrina. "Everyone knows how organized you are."

"But am I organized enough for Mr. McRyan?" I asked. I put on my best imitation of Mr. McRyan, with his southern accent and huge vocabulary. "Have I contemplated all the necessities of this here endeavor?"

Sabrina and Allie laughed, but my little voice asked, *Well, have you?*

I didn't want to go to drama the next day. I thought for sure that everyone would still be teasing me about flatulence. But I forgot everything when I walked into the room and saw the note on the board.

TWENTY-TWO SLOTS LEFT FOR THE BROADWAY TRIP!

"How are the slots going so quickly?" I said to Mrs. Alamantia. "It's only been a few days!"

"I guess everyone is excited," said Mrs. Alamantia.

"The shows are really good," I said. "I just thought I had more time." I took a deep breath and tried not to panic, but the words were in big capital letters, like they were shouting at me. TWENTY-TWO SLOTS LEFT FOR THE BROADWAY TRIP! Mrs. Alamantia had five drama classes; if just a couple of kids in each class brought in their deposit, those slots could be gone in an instant.

There's a song from the musical *Rent* called "Seasons of Love" that talks about how there are 525,600 minutes in a year. It sounds inspiring on the one hand, but on the other hand, you realize that all those minutes pass and we barely realize it. I wondered how many minutes I had.

Henry came in and looked at the board. "Does that mean we can stop talking about this trip all the time?" he asked. I wanted to slug him.

"Have you ever actually been to a Broadway show?" asked Mrs. Alamantia. "Gotten dressed up, waited for the lights to go down, and savored that moment when a hush falls over everything right before the curtain goes up?" Mrs. A was describing one of my favorite parts of going to a show.

Henry half smiled, so his stupid dimple showed. "No, I haven't," he admitted.

"Don't knock it till you try it," said Mrs. Alamantia. "It's just one of the greatest human creations on earth, gathering together to tell a story. And about so many things! There's a Broadway show about the French Revolution, about cats, about Hamilton—"

"Everyone knows about that one," announced Henry.

"Don't interrupt," I said. "That's rude."

Henry lifted one eyebrow and didn't say anything for a moment. Then he turned to Mrs. Alamantia. "I'm sorry I interrupted," he said. He actually sounded like he meant it.

"Not a problem. You probably kept me from naming every Broadway show I've ever loved," said Mrs. Alamantia.

"Some people don't *appreciate* Broadway," I said, glaring

at Henry's back as he sat down. But I did. I definitely appreciated Broadway!

· •.• 🧃 •.• ·

When I got home from school, I thought Dad wasn't home because the car was gone. But Dad was inside, trying to teach Phineas how to stop barking by using K-99.

"Yip. Yip, yip, yip!" squeaked K-99. "Yip! Yi—"

"K-99, quiet!!" said Dad. K-99 quieted down. Then Dad pushed a button that made a doorbell sound. Phineas started barking.

"Quiet, Phineas," said Dad. Phineas kept barking. Dad repeated the command. Phineas stared at the door and barked more loudly. I covered my ears. He was so loud!

I opened the door. "There's no one there, see?" I said to Phineas. Phineas stopped barking and looked at me. I patted him on the head. "Good boy."

"He's supposed to learn from K-99," said Dad.

"But he was making my ears ring with his barking," I

said. "And he stopped." Phineas sat down and looked from me to Dad, then back to me.

"I'll find a way," said Dad. "If you want to find a way, you will find a way."

Dad looked like he was going to try the doorbell again, so I interrupted him. "Where's the car?"

"The car?" Dad looked puzzled for a minute. Dad was definitely in one of his deep-in-work modes, when the rest of the world disappeared. "Oh yeah. The car is in the shop."

"What's wrong with it?" I asked.

Dad chuckled. "What, were you planning to go for a drive?"

I tried not to look panicked. I knew enough that car repairs were not cheap.

"I think it's the transmission," said Dad. "The guy said he'd call me in a few hours." Dad put his arm around me. "Don't worry, though I know you will. We're all stocked up on groceries, and I don't need to go anywhere. If we need anything, we can walk or ride our bikes."

Dad thought I was worried about not having a car. But it was worse than that—a transmission repair definitely sounded expensive. Maybe I'd have to earn money so we could keep the car!

The Dog Rearranged My Homework

On Friday night, Dad and I made pizza and plans for the weekend. Normally, it was one of my favorite times of the week because the whole weekend seemed ready for all sorts of possibilities. But this weekend, I had to get my notebook ready for Mr. McRyan's notebook check, and I was going to ask Dad for help in finding some babysitting.

I carefully spread the pepperoni pieces over the whole pizza so they were evenly distributed, and I set the table. I waited until the pizza was in the oven and Dad was making the salad. I cleared my throat and said, "So, I was thinking of doing some babysitting."

Dad stopped in the middle of tossing the salad. "You want to babysit? You?"

I squirmed in my seat. "Yeah. What's wrong with that?"

"Well, on numerous occasions, you have declared small children to be filthy, sticky, germy, gross, and disgusting. And that's when you were still a small child yourself," said Dad. "I just figured you weren't going to be into babysitting. I know your mom wasn't."

"She wasn't?" I loved finding out these little dollops of information about Mom.

"Nope. But somehow, that didn't stop her from wanting her own children, and here you are, the neatest, tidiest child we could have imagined." Dad laughed. "So why the sudden interest in babysitting?"

"It's not *sudden*," I said guiltily. "I just think it would be good to have a job, learn some responsibility."

"Well, I can ask around. I'm sure someone would love your help," said Dad. He sprinkled some goat cheese on top of the salad and then tossed a chunk to Phineas. Phineas gulped the whole piece down and looked hopefully at Dad for more. "What else is on the agenda?"

"I have to get my notebook ready for Mr. McRyan's notebook check," I said.

"Oh, I'm sure your notebook is fine," said Dad. "That's one thing I never have to worry about with you, Chloe."

I don't want you to have to worry about anything with me, I thought. "No, Dad, you don't understand. Mr. McRyan's notebook checks are legendarily hard. He has *failed* people."

The timer dinged, and Dad took a peek in the oven. "I'm going to give it another few minutes," Dad announced. "Look, Chloe, let's say you did fail. I'd go in and talk to Mr. McRyan and see what was going on."

"But isn't it better to just not have the bad thing happen?" I asked.

"Well, sure, but I don't want you to turn yourself into a pretzel, either," said Dad. "Sometimes a person can get so busy making sure things don't happen that they don't let a marvelous mess happen, either."

"Marvelous mess?" I said. "Isn't that like saying a fabulous basement flood?" Dad kept his workshop in the basement, which did flood once.

"I mean, something good that happens when you don't expect it," said Dad. "Maybe even when something unpleasant is happening. Like me meeting Mom because I got lost in the hospital."

"And then it turned out you guys were headed to the same place," I said, remembering. "Radiology."

"That's a marvelous mess," said Dad. "Maybe I could have planned my way beforehand and checked the maps, but instead I met Mom."

"I don't think there are any marvelous messes when it comes to Mr. McRyan," I told Dad.

I decided to work on my notebook first thing on Saturday morning, while everything was fresh and quiet. The rings in the binder weren't closing all the way, so I took all the papers out of the binder and set them on the floor into the different categories Mr. McRyan wanted. Notes, tests, projects.

Dad poked his head in. "Whoa. That's a lot of paper."

"I told you," I said, pulling out a new yellow binder. "Everything has to be perfect, *and* Mr. McRyan does not believe in digital anything." I started to hold up the stack of Mr. McRyan's notes when I saw it. "Look!"

Dad stared at the notes on the Great Depression. "What's wrong?"

"What's wrong? Do you see that spot? That's from Phineas slobbering over the five causes of the Great Depression!" Maybe I would have to rewrite it.

Dad squinted. "Aw, Chloe, you can barely see it. And it's not like you can't read the writing. It's all still legible."

"This is the type of stuff I could get dinged on! That

dumb dog!" I threw my head back and shouted, "Phineas!" Immediately I heard the rhythmic thud of Phineas running down the hall and realized my mistake.

"No, no, no!" I leaned forward, trying to protect the papers. But I was no match for Phineas. Phineas barreled into me, sending me and all the papers across the room. "You dumb dog!" I shouted as the papers fluttered around me. "Look at what you did."

"Phinny thought you were calling him, and he got all excited," explained Dad. Phineas sat on a pile of papers and panted happily. He started wagging his tail, which sent more papers into the air. "No! Phineas! No!" I glared at Dad. "This is not a marvelous mess! This is a doggy disaster!"

"Sometimes messes are just messes. Try to be calm." Dad took Phineas out of the room, then came back inside and shut the door. "Now you can clean up in peace."

All my neat stacks had been decimated. I felt like crying. "This is going to take forever to fix!" Panic rose in my chest. "My papers are all messed up. I'm going to fail the notebook check. I won't get into a good college . . ."

"One step at a time," said Dad. He crouched down next to me and helped collect papers. "Fixing your notebook will take longer than you expected, but you can do it. And your grades in middle school don't count for college, anyway." He handed me some papers. "Do you want me to clear the dining room table?"

"Can I go somewhere to work?" I asked.

"Like where?" asked Dad.

My first choice was the library, but it wouldn't open until noon. I wanted to work *now*.

"The boba shop," I decided. "They like people who work quietly. And dogs are not allowed." Dad opened the door, and Phineas came back in, still oblivious to the damage he had caused. He nudged my hand for a pet, rattling the papers I was holding.

Dad put a hand on Phineas, rubbing his neck. "He didn't do it on purpose."

"I know, but still." I gestured to all the papers. "Now I have to redo all of this." I thought about the *Billy Elliot* angry dance. *Billy Elliot* is a musical about a boy who wants to dance ballet against his father's wishes; the angry dance involves a lot of screaming and stompy dancing. I wanted to do the same thing, except organize instead of dance.

"Okay, okay, go," said Dad. He scratched his head. "Is this a bad time to mention that Auntie Sue wants you to call her?"

It's a great time, snarked my little voice. *All the terrible things at once!*

"I'll call her," I said. I didn't want to make the Auntie Sue thing harder for Dad. But this weekend was going downhill in a hurry!

Tea Palace was quiet; just a few people were working at their laptops or reading the newspaper. Henry was unpacking a box of napkins, but when he saw me, he told the other person that he'd take my order.

"Are you going to order a real drink this time?" Henry teased.

"A soda is a real drink," I said.

"Oh, you know what I mean," said Henry. "What are you doing here so early, anyway?"

I reached into my backpack and pulled out the stack of Phineas-ly arranged papers. Henry's eyes widened. "You must be an imposter. The Chloe I know would never allow that to happen," he said.

"The dog decided to 'help' me organize my notebook for Mr. McRyan's class," I said sourly. "I need a quiet place to get everything sorted out."

"Well, okay, you've come to the perfect place. You just need the perfect drink to keep you company," said Henry.

"Let's see," I said. "The perfect drink would cheer me up because the dog messed up my notebook, help me focus on fixing my notebook, and give me the strength I need to call my aunt."

"It's a lot to ask of a drink," said Henry. "But fortunately for you, I have just the thing. You need a Thai milk tea."

"Thai tea? *Thai* tea? Boba is from Taiwan, not Thailand," I said.

"We don't discriminate," said Henry. "We support all the Asians. And are you always this demanding, or am I just lucky?"

"I'm only this way around people who need to be taken down a peg. Or three," I said.

"So, one Thai tea?" persisted Henry. *Make that seventeen pegs.*

"Okay," I said. "That's one option."

"It's the only option," said Henry. "The only good one for this exact situation." Henry pressed his palms against the counter and leaned forward. His eyes twinkled. "Trust me; I'm a professional."

I gave Henry a doubtful look. "And if you're wrong?"

"I won't be," said Henry. "Thai tea has caffeine so you can focus, but it's sweet so it will cheer you up. And there's this nutty flavor that, I don't know, makes you feel you can do anything. Like call difficult aunts. But"—Henry took a breath—"in the unlikely case that you think I'm wrong, I'll replace your drink for free."

I looked at the menu board—it really didn't have anything else I wanted to order. "Fine," I said. "One Thai tea, please." *And if there's anything remotely wrong with it, I'm telling you.*

"Here you go," said Henry, handing me the drink.

"Wait, how did that come up so fast?" I asked.

"I'd already put in the order," said Henry, smiling.

"What if I had gone with a different drink?" I demanded.

"But you didn't," said Henry.

"But I could have," I said.

Henry shrugged. "I guess I would have gotten a Thai tea for my break drink!"

I thought about what my dad had said about marvelous messes. It seemed like Henry was going out of his way to make a mess happen, happy or not. But that wasn't the worst part.

The worst part was that it was perfect. Cold and sweet. After the first sip, I felt ready to tackle the notebook, and anything else that came my way.

"How is it?" asked Henry. He was practically gloating.

"It's adequate," I said. I was kicking myself for not waiting to take a sip until I was out of Henry's sight.

"You're welcome!" called Henry as I walked away.

I decided to start with the notebook and finish with calling Auntie Sue. The notebook wasn't as hard as I thought it would be because I had already had a highlighter system for the different units and types of papers. At one point, Henry walked by and said, "Nice notebook."

"Thank you," I said. "I have a color system for all my classes."

"So yellow for . . . social studies?"

"Correct," I said.

"Maybe I should do something like that," said Henry. "Right now, all my notebooks are black."

"Well, how do you keep track of your classes?" I asked.

"Your question has a big assumption built into it," said Henry. "I prefer the fly-by-the-seat-of-my-pants method."

Just hearing Henry describe his lack of organization made my stomach tighten up. "Do you at least study for tests?"

"This word you use, *study*. I am not familiar with it," said Henry with a fake accent. "How to explain this?"

"Please stop," I said. I wasn't sure if I was going to start laughing or screaming. "I don't understand how you live."

Henry stopped talking, tilted his head, and smiled.

"Why are you looking at me like that?" I said.

"I think more people live like me than you; that's all," said Henry, still smiling. "I think you're the one to wonder about."

The way Henry was looking at me was making me feel weird. "I, um, have to make a phone call." Henry nodded and walked back to the counter.

I dialed Auntie Sue's phone number, hoping that I could just leave a message. No such luck.

"CHLOE! HOW IS MY FAVORITE NIECE?" Auntie Sue sounded like she was shouting into the phone. The people sitting around the table turned their heads in my direction.

I lowered my voice, hoping that she would follow my lead. "I'm fine," I whispered. "How are you?"

"IS SOMETHING WRONG? ARE YOU SICK? DO YOU NEED ME TO COME RIGHT NOW? I'M IN THE CAR." I frantically pressed the down volume button on my phone, but not before Henry's uncle caught my eye and pointed to the sign about being quiet. I nodded and covered the phone with my hand.

"I'm fine, Auntie Sue," I said. "I'm not sick; I'm just at a boba shop, so I have to speak quietly. How are you?" I held my hand over the phone and hoped that would be enough.

"OH, BUSY. YOU KNOW. ALWAYS A DEAL TO MAKE." I'm sure Auntie Sue thought she had lowered her voice, but now it just sounded like regular shouting instead of a supersonic boom. Aunt Sue worked in commercial real estate. Usually, at some point, she was going to remind me that she was the number one broker in her area. "BUT I'M NOT TOO BUSY FOR YOU! I WANT TO COME SEE YOU. MAKE SURE YOUR FATHER IS NOT LETTING YOU STARVE TO DEATH."

"Dad can cook," I reminded her in a slightly louder voice.

"I'M KIDDING, I'M KIDDING. I WANT TO SPEND TIME WITH MY FAVORITE NIECE. ARE YOU AVAILABLE ON THURSDAY AFTER SCHOOL? I HAVE A MEETING NEAR YOU. WE CAN GET BOBA." Henry's uncle was heading back in my direction. "OTHERWISE, I CAN COME ON SATURDAY OR SUNDAY OR . . ." I needed to end this conversation now. I didn't even look at my calendar.

"Yes-yes-Thursday-sounds-great-I've-got-to-go-now!" I half whispered, half yelped into my phone. "See-you-soon-bye!" I hit the end button just as the angriest man in Tea Palace arrived at my table.

"We do not encourage phone calls at Tea Palace," he said gruffly, which was actually a nicer reaction than I expected.

"Sorry," I whispered. "It's my aunt. She, um, wants to make sure I can hear her."

"The whole café could hear her," said Henry's uncle.

"It won't happen again," I promised.

"When are you bringing your aunt here?!" called Henry from behind the counter.

I was already regretting my decision to see Auntie Sue.

Mary Poppins Never Had to Deal with Legos

I knocked on the door and a boy with big brown eyes and curly hair opened it and stared up at me. He was wearing a red-and-blue-striped T-shirt. "Hi," I began, saying the words I had long dreaded. "I'm Chloe, your babysitter."

Dad had gotten in touch with Mrs. Mansfield, who was looking for a babysitter for her five-year-old twins, George and Ellis. The way I figured it, five was a good age to babysit. Five-year-olds seemed pretty sturdy. They didn't need diapers or baby food or anything like that. My cousin Millicent was five, and she was pretty independent. I just had to keep the twins entertained and uninjured for two or three hours. That seemed doable. And Mrs. Mansfield paid fifteen dollars an hour, which seemed like a pretty good deal.

Sabrina's advice? Stay one step ahead. Don't show fear, but don't be scary. Snacks can take a long time.

"What's your name?" I asked the little boy. I took a quick look at his hands and noticed that they looked clean and unsticky. A good sign.

The boy ducked his head behind the door and peered back out. "Ellis," he said shyly. He drew out the sound, so it sounded like he was saying *Ellllllllll-is.*

"We're gonna have fun," I told him. "But I have to talk to your mom first."

Ellis ran off into the house, leaving me standing by the

door. I wasn't sure if I should let myself in, or if I should just stand there, but then Mrs. Mansfield appeared at the door. She seemed really excited to see me.

"Chloe! Great, you're here! I have to run into the office and get a few things done," she said. She spoke quickly, putting some files and a charger in a bag while she spoke to me. "You've met Ellis, right? Let me introduce you to George, and then we'll be all set. George!!!"

A small figure skidded into the kitchen. "Yes, Mom?" He looked just like Ellis, right down to the same red-and-blue-striped T-shirt. I guessed Mrs. Mansfield was one of those moms who liked to dress her twins in identical clothes.

"This is Chloe; she's going to watch you while I go into the office. You listen to her, okay? Be a good boy," she said. "You guys have to clean up your room, and then you can go outside and play. I have mandarin oranges, carrots, and Goldfish crackers if they get hungry. They're in an orange phase. My number is on the fridge if you need it." She waved and headed out the door.

"Where's your brother?" I asked George. "He was just here."

"I dunno," said George, shrugging. "Somewhere. Wanna see our room?"

"Well, what about Ellis?"

"He'll show up," said George confidently. "But I want to show you our room." He was already walking down the hallway.

"Okay," I said, following. I guessed little kids liked showing off their bedrooms. I hoped it wasn't too bad. The part of the house I had seen so far wasn't messy, just lived in.

"Ta-da!" George opened the door and flung open his arms. I tried not to scream. I couldn't even see the *floor*, it was so covered in toys and clothes. The bunk bed seemed to be shedding blankets and pillows. I saw five shoes, none matching.

"You guys have a lot of stuff," I said faintly. *Maybe Ellis was buried in a toy avalanche*, suggested my little voice. *And you're going to be blamed for it.*

"You wanna play Legos?" asked George. He started to

walk over to the closet door, stepping on several piles of clothes along the way.

"I don't think we should take anything else out until the room gets picked up," I said. I pushed my feet along the floor, shoving toys out of the way as I went. A dark green carpet began to emerge. "And where's Ellis?" Would it count as babysitting two kids if I only ever saw one?

George didn't answer. He started to open the closet door. There was so much stuff on the floor that he couldn't open the door the whole way. I sighed and went over to help him. Maybe he'd listen to me once he had the Legos.

"Rawwwr!" Suddenly, the door flew open. I screamed and jumped back. So much for not showing fear.

A boy in a green-and-blue-striped shirt jumped out of the closet and screamed, "Boo!" Then he and George started laughing so hard that they fell on the floor.

"Who are you?" I asked, trying to catch my breath.

"I'm George!" said the boy in the green-and-blue shirt. "We tricked you! We tricked you and Mommy!"

"You met me twice!" said Ellis proudly. "And you didn't even know."

"Once as yourself, and once as George," I said, half to myself, half to the boys. Ellis covered his mouth with his hands and giggled. His eyes were shining.

"Huh," I said. "That's a good one!" A plan began to form in my mind.

"You're not mad?" asked George. He seemed disappointed.

"This room is so messy it definitely seemed like a possibility that a monster could live here," I said. "But it's a solid prank." I stuck out my hand and high-fived each boy.

"We switch at school all the time, and nobody knows," said Ellis proudly. "Except our best friends."

"How do I know you're telling me the truth?" I asked. "Maybe you're still messing with me."

"Oh!" George turned around and started tugging on his pants. "Because Mom marks our underwe—"

"Nope! Stop! I believe you! I totally believe you," I said. I looked from one boy to the other. I really could not find any distinguishing characteristics besides their shirts. Maybe George was a *little* taller, but that was it.

"Whaddaya want to do now?" asked George.

"Mom said we had to clean our room," said Ellis.

George shrugged. "Okay." He lowered his hands and, like a snowplow, began to shove toys to the side.

"What are you doing?" I said.

"That's what Mom means when she says to clean our room," said George. "She just wants a clear path to the bunk bed."

"That's not what she really wants," Ellis told me. "It's just that if we do that, she won't get mad. She'll just sigh and say we should do a better job later."

"Why don't you do a good job?" I asked.

"It takes too long," whined George. "It would take foreeeeever."

I scanned the room. It was messy, but it wasn't dirty. "How about this? I think we can get this room really clean in thirteen minutes. If you promise to work hard for thirteen minutes, then I promise that we'll stop if we're not done after that time. But we should be done."

The twins had a quick meeting. "How long is thirteen minutes?" asked Ellis.

"It takes fifteen minutes to walk to school," said George. "So it's less than that." Ellis nodded.

"Okay," I said. "You have to do exactly as I say." The twins nodded. "When I say go, start by pulling up the sheets and bedspreads on your beds, okay. *But not before then.* We have to stay exactly within thirteen minutes."

"Can we be on our beds?" asked George.

"Yes, but you can't start making them until I say go." I set up the timer on my phone and then yelled, "Go!"

Making the bed is one of my big hacks—it's the biggest thing in the room, and when it's clean, the whole room seems better. The boys quickly took care of the sheets and bedspreads; George even smoothed his pillow.

The clothes were the next line of attack.

"You're done with the beds. Scoop up the clothes and put

'em in the hamper," I instructed. The boys piled clothes into the hamper until it looked like a mountain, but that was okay—it was better than the clothes being on the floor. "Give it a smush if you have to." Ellis reached up and squashed the clothes down with his hands.

"Thirty seconds for shoes," I said. "See how many pairs you can find. *Matching* pairs," I said. I counted down from thirty. Shoes began to appear from out of nowhere. Sneakers, soccer cleats, rain boots, and brown leather shoes. George found five pairs; Ellis found three. I had them line up the shoes by the hamper. They were breathing hard.

"How much time is left?" asked Ellis. I checked my phone. Six minutes and seventeen seconds.

"We're going to divide and conquer now," I told them. "George, you're in charge of toys and books. Put the toys in the toy box and the books on the shelves. Ellis, you're in charge of putting away the games and stacking them up."

"Why do I get two things and Ellis only gets one?" asked George.

"Because it takes more effort to put the pieces in the boxes," I said.

"Do you want to switch?" asked Ellis.

"No," said George quickly. They got to work. I helped Ellis find the pieces that went with different games. We stacked Operation, Battleship, checkers, and Jenga in a neat pile just as George put the last book on the shelf.

"Okay! We're done!" I said. I clapped my hands. The room looked so much better. Not like something in a magazine, but also nothing like a disaster movie.

"Whoaaaa!" said Ellis, looking around appreciatively. "Mom is going to freak out!"

"We have so much space now!" said George. He ran out of the room, holding his arms out. "Wooow!"

"See?" I said. "It didn't take that long. And now we can go outside and play!"

"Well, I want to play here," said George, pointing to the empty space we had just created. I tried not to shudder at the thought of all our work getting undone. But Ellis jumped in before I could say anything.

"We can play here," said Ellis. "But we have to put everything back."

"Well, of course," said George, as if that was the most obvious thing in the world. The boys first thought they wanted to play with Legos but then decided to build a marble race course.

"These Legos are kind of sticky," said Ellis.

"Maybe that's something else you can clean," I said. "See, once you have a habit of keeping things clean, you want everything to be clean." Ellis nodded and walked into the hallway with the Legos. I was about to ask where he was going when George jumped up and pointed a finger at me.

"Hey!" he said. "You tricked us!"

"Tricked you?" I asked. "About what?"

"Cleaning!" he said. He flung his arms out to the side.

"I told you you were cleaning," I said. "There's no trick about it. It's not like you thought you were, I don't know, eating marshmallows."

"No," said George indignantly. "But you made us like it!"

"I promise I wasn't trying to trick you. I just know that I like knowing how long a chore will last, so I figured it was better to put a time limit on it. And, well, I like making things clean, so I guess some of that rubbed off on you guys," I said.

"It was a trick," grumbled George.

"I didn't intend for it to be a trick, even though I kind of owed you guys one," I said. "For the prank you played on me. I just don't think cleaning has to be some terrible chore that makes people grumpy."

George seemed to think about that for a while. "Like *Mary Poppins*," he said. I knew what he was talking about. He was talking about the scene where Mary Poppins sings "A Spoonful of Sugar" and the room seems to clean itself. I remember being amazed by the things she seemed to pull from her carpetbag—a coatrack, a lamp, a huge leafy plant.

"Did you like *Mary Poppins*?" I asked. Maybe the boys liked musicals—I could definitely make that work.

"It was okay," said George. "But there weren't any explosions."

"There was a cannon that went off!" I protested. "Admiral Boom!"

"Not any *good* explosions," complained George.

"Well, anyway, I don't have magic," I said. "We just cleaned the room in a fun way."

"Could you . . . ?" started George. I wondered if he was going to ask if I could get some magic.

"Could I what?"

"Could you write down what you did so we can do it again when you're not here?" asked George softly. "Like, make a list and tape it to the wall? You have to print because we haven't learned cursive yet."

"Of course," I said. Maybe babysitting wasn't so bad. Maybe I could make my Broadway money! "You bet."

When Mrs. Mansfield got home, we were trying to set up the Mouse Trap game on the floor of the boys' bedroom. She walked in and gasped.

"What's going on here? I can see the floor? And the beds are made?"

"You said the boys had to clean up their room before they could play," I said. Mrs. Mansfield sounded so unnerved I was starting to worry that she meant something else.

"That usually means they hide their toys under the bed," she said. "This is *miraculous*."

"We put away our clothes, and made the bed, and put away the games . . ." said George, counting off each job on his fingers. "And, uh, put books on the bookshelf."

"And I washed the Legos!" added Ellis proudly.

"You did? When did you do that?" I asked. I looked around for the bucket of Legos I had seen before. They were gone.

"They were sticky," said Ellis.

"That's why you washed the Legos," said Mrs. Mansfield, smiling. "Not when."

"Or how," I added. "We've been together practically the whole time."

Ellis's lower lip trembled. "You made cleaning fun," he said. "So I was trying to find other ways to clean and have fun."

"What's that sound?" asked Mrs. Mansfield. When the boys had been playing, I hadn't noticed other noises in the house. But now it filled our ears like a roar.

This Is a Drill

Mrs. Alamantia had a new note on the board when I got to school the next day. FIFTEEN SLOTS LEFT FOR THE BROADWAY TRIP.

Henry came over to me. "Do you need me to read that to you? You've been staring at it for a long time."

"I can read it just fine," I said. "I'm trying to earn money for the trip, but it's not going great."

"Have you tried—" started Henry.

"If you say babysitting, I will scream. Loudly." Henry

closed his mouth. "I did try babysitting. It was a complete and total disaster. I destroyed a family's clothes washer. Water and Legos everywhere." I thought Henry might make fun of me, or say that missing Broadway was no big deal, but he didn't.

"Um, I don't want to make you feel bad, but Legos are not supposed—" said Henry.

"Yes, of course I know that you don't put Legos in a washer!" I said. "The kid didn't."

"Do I want to know how he got that idea?"

"I was babysitting twins, and I got them to clean up their room in a really fun way," I explained. "One of them got so excited that he dumped all his Legos in the washing machine because he wanted them to be clean, too. And I was talking to the other one, who thought I had tricked them into thinking cleaning up was fun, so I missed the whole thing."

Henry put his hand over his mouth, but I could still tell from his eyes that he was smiling.

"It's not funny," I said. "I need to make money. I bet that mom is probably telling everyone not to hire me."

"I dunno." Henry scratched the back of his neck. "Seems to me that if you've got a kid who's going to do something like that, you're kinda used to stuff breaking."

"She did pretty much say that," I admitted. "But she made a lot of sad sounds before she got to that point."

Henry started to say something, but then Mrs. Alamantia came over and asked if I was planning to go on the trip.

"I want to go," I said. "I mean, I really, really want to go. But I have to earn enough money, and I'm not sure I have enough time." I could feel my throat close up a bit when I said that. Talking to Henry had calmed me down a little, but now I had to take a deep breath so I wouldn't cry.

Mrs. Alamantia put her hand on top of mine. "We have this trip every year, so you can always put your money toward next year's trip. But you're a smart girl; you'll find a way, I bet."

Isabel Zhang walked up to Mrs. Alamantia and handed

her a piece of paper. "This is last week's assignment," she said. "Sorry it's late. I couldn't find it."

Mrs. Alamantia sighed. "I'll have to mark it down, I'm afraid, though it's better than missing the assignment completely." She turned to me. "I don't understand why you guys give away points by turning things in late."

"My parents will kill me if I get a B in drama," said Isabel. "Or anything, for that matter."

Mrs. Alamantia pointed her chin at me. "Chloe never turns anything in late." This happens all the time. Teachers think they're complimenting me, instead of calling me out for my nerd-tastic tendencies. It's kind of embarrassing, even though it's true.

"Oh yeah," said Isabel. She put a hand on her hip. "Clutterless Chloe, keeping things clean. Are you ready for Mr. McRyan's notebook check?" The way Isabel talked, she sounded like she was in charge, instead of the one in trouble.

"I think so. I double-checked all the assignments against

the agenda again this morning," I said. "And I have all my tests and corrections."

"Oh, Mr. McRyan's infamous notebook checks," said Mrs. Alamantia. She waved her hands in the air. "I usually know when it's happening based on the number of students who are crying."

"Everyone's betting that if anyone does well, it will be Chloe," said Isabel.

"You won't go wrong, betting on Chloe," said Mrs. Alamantia. Isabel gave me a funny smile. "Clutterless Chloe," she repeated, cocking her head to one side.

The way Mr. McRyan conducted the notebook checks was he called you up to his desk, one by one in alphabetical order by last name, looked through your notebook, and told you what your grade was. You did not get to argue with him or get a chance to look for a missing paper. His word was final.

Laurel Knauss got a D-minus, which was as close as you could come to failing without actually failing. She cried quietly at her desk, though I wasn't surprised. Whenever Laurel opened her backpack, a few papers would fall out. Mr. McRyan called her notebook *calamitous*. She was a friend of Isabel's—I wondered if she would tell Isabel what happened. It took Mr. McRyan a long time to get to the *W*s.

Ryan Walker did a fist pump after he got his grade. We all asked him what he'd gotten. Ryan was really smart. He was already taking high school math.

"A C-plus!" said Ryan excitedly. "I thought I was going to fail." My seatmate, Carly, and I looked at each other open-mouthed. Carly had gotten a C. This was not good.

"Chloe Wong," called Mr. McRyan.

I stood up, feeling my legs wobble. I walked up to the front of the room, where Mr. McRyan's desk was, and laid my notebook in front of him.

Mr. McRyan opened the notebook to the first page, where I had put the class syllabus.

"Huh!" He actually made a noise, though I couldn't tell if he was mad or surprised or both. I had put the syllabus in a page protector so it wouldn't get ratty during the year. Maybe I wasn't supposed to do that.

Mr. McRyan flipped to the middle of the notebook, which brought him to our section on citizenship. He looked at the glossary I had written up and then highlighted according to whether the term was economic, civic, or geographic.

"Hmph!" This sound was even more ambiguous than the previous one. Maybe he was annoyed that I had used so many different highlighters. Mr. McRyan had a lot of pet peeves, which he probably had built up over many, many years of teaching. He only liked blue ballpoint pens, not black, and he got really angry if we said *like* too many times in class.

Finally, Mr. McRyan flipped to the end of the notebook. This was where I kept all the weekly quizzes. I peeked over his shoulder and tried not to gasp. Somehow, I had completely missed a quiz with a missing piece at the bottom. The missing piece was in the exact shape of a dog bite, a Phineas-shaped bite, to be specific.

How could Phineas have been so stupid? How could *I* have been so stupid? This was probably the sort of thing Mr. McRyan failed people for. I closed my eyes and waited for his verdict.

"Chloe," said Mr. McRyan. "I don't do this very often . . ."

But I am going to give you an F-minus, my little voice helpfully filled in.

"But I believe this notebook is worthy of an A-minus," finished Mr. McRyan.

"What?" The class gasped along with me. Technically, we were not supposed to listen to one another's grades, but we couldn't help it.

"Oh, I know, it's probably an A." Mr. McRyan chuckled. "But you have to have something to work for in the second semester." He handed me my notebook and winked.

"Thank you," I breathed. As I walked back to my seat, people began sticking out their hands, asking to see the notebook, but I had crossed my arms over it, not daring to let go just yet.

"Did you really . . . ?" Carly began to ask. But before she could get out the rest of the question, a loud squawking sound filled the room, and an orange light began to flash on and off. We were having a fire drill.

"Leave your things. We're going to parking lot C to line up," said Mr. McRyan. "Let's go."

The thing about fire drills is that, chances are, it's just that—it's practice. But there's always a tiny part of my brain that wonders if it's a real emergency. A disaster.

"I thought I smelled smoke," whispered Carly. We weren't supposed to be talking, but everyone did. "Did you smell smoke? Or something kind of chemical-y?"

"I didn't," I said. "But maybe I missed it."

"The kids coming out of the gym said the air was hazy in the locker room," said Ryan.

"That's from the BO," joked Laurel.

"Straight line, face away from the building," said Mr. McRyan. "No talking." We were supposed to face away from the building in case it exploded, which never made sense to me. Wouldn't we want to see if any debris was coming our way so we could duck?

My insides felt like they were twisting tighter and tighter. I wanted to know if this was an emergency or not. Maybe I should call my dad so he wouldn't worry, even though we weren't supposed to use our phones during school hours. I hunched over. My stomach hurt.

"It's just a fire drill." A class had lined up next to ours, and Henry had ended up next to me.

"How do you know that for sure?" I asked.

Henry scanned the throngs of kids and teachers around us. "I mean . . . it's not a field trip."

"No, I mean how do you know it's a drill, and not a real emergency?" I asked.

"Okay, so let's assume it's the worst-case scenario, and there is a real fire," said Henry. "Everyone is out of the building. Look, Mrs. Kirby has even brought out Linguini and Bucatini." Mrs. Kirby was one of the science teachers.

Linguini and Bucatini were snakes. "So, the people are safe, which is the most important thing." Henry turned and studied the building, even though we were supposed to face away from it. "I see Ms. Valdez, the vice principal. She seems pretty relaxed, which is not her normal state. Look, she's smiling. I think we're okay." There was something about the way Henry talked that felt nice, like a warm cup of hot cocoa. Or taro milk tea.

"Maybe Ms. Valdez is one of those people who gets calmer in an emergency," I said. My mom was like that. Everyone in the ER loved her because she never shouted. She just knew what to do.

"Okay, kids, we're going back in!" Mrs. Alamantia walked by and winked at me. She put her arm up in the air. "Head back in, please! No running!"

"See?" said Henry. "Nothing to worry about."

"You were right . . . this time . . ." I said. Henry gave me his one-dimple smile as his class moved away. As we walked back into the building, I realized I was smiling, too.

Mr. McRyan told us to pack up and then wait for the announcement that we could go to the next class. We were going to skip sixth period and go straight to seventh. He told us he didn't want a "brouhaha," which is a word that I have only ever heard Mr. McRyan say.

Carly noticed before me. She pointed to the empty spot in front of my seat and said, "Did you take your notebook with you?"

"What? No!" I looked around my seat, on the floor, even in my backpack, though I was pretty sure I had not put it away.

I raised my hand. "Mr. McRyan, my notebook . . ." An announcement came over the PA, drowning out my voice. I raised my hand frantically.

"Chloe, we can deal with it tomorrow," said Mr. McRyan. "The next class is getting ready to come in."

"My notebook . . ." I said desperately.

"It can wait until tomorrow," said Mr. McRyan firmly.

Maybe in all the confusion someone had taken my notebook by accident. Part of me wanted to throw myself across the door and ask to check everyone's bags. Insist on finding my notebook.

But that would be making a scene. A mess.

I was one of the last kids in the classroom to leave. And the only one to leave without my notebook.

Confrontation at the Tea Palace

"So you got an A-minus on Mr. McRyan's notebook check and someone stole it?" asked Sabrina after school.

"I don't think someone stole it," I said, shocked that she had used that word. "Someone must have taken it by accident."

"Come on," said Sabrina. "You have that crazy color scheme. How many people have bright yellow notebooks? Your notebook was stolen." I nodded my head, reluctantly. Sabrina was right.

"I tried to tell Mr. McRyan, but he said it had to wait until tomorrow." I didn't say the rest. I should have said something. Shouted *stop* and made everyone listen to me. But I couldn't do it.

"It was probably someone in your class. That's pretty daring," said Sabrina.

"That's what doesn't make sense," I said. "I'm at the end of the alphabet. Everyone else already got a grade."

"That notebook became an instant legend," said Sabrina. "I mean, you got an A-minus in Mr. McRyan's class."

"My next grade is going to be an F because I won't have the notebook," I said.

"Oh, come on," said Sabrina. "Even Mr. McRyan will understand. He won't ding you for that."

"I'm glad you're so certain," I said.

"What I don't get is, it's your stuff. In your handwriting, with your color coding and all that other stuff you do," said Sabrina. "No one can try to pass that off as their own."

I let out a long, noisy sigh.

Sabrina linked her arm through mine. "You know what you need?"

"My social studies notebook?"

Sabrina laughed. "Okay, you know what else you need? You need a boba."

And maybe you can see Henry! said the little voice in my head. My little voice was getting out of hand. Why should I be excited about seeing Henry?

Henry was not working at the counter when Sabrina and I went in—*not that I care, anyway,* I reminded my little voice. Sabrina ordered a coconut milk tea. I didn't know what to order. What would Henry say? What did you order when everything seemed so wrong? Finally, I picked a mango slush.

"Mango day, huh?" asked Sabrina.

"The color reminds me of my notebook," I told her. "My missing notebook." I took a sip, hoping the bright citrus flavor would cheer me up.

Sabrina led the way to a table near a window with bamboo plants in small pots on the sill. "Oh, look, there are some kids from school!" Sabrina waved. I knew some of the kids, including Isabel and Laurel. They had been talking, but when they saw me, they went quiet and exchanged looks.

"That's funny," said Sabrina.

"What's funny?"

Sabrina put her drink down on the table and gestured for me to follow her. "Hi, guys," said Sabrina. If you knew Sabrina the way I did, you'd know that this was not her sincere, friendly tone. "What's up?"

"Nothing," said Isabel. "Just hanging out. How about you?"

"We were celebrating Chloe's notebook grade. Did you hear? McRyan gave her an A-minus. I think the last person who got close to that grade started Twitter or something," said Sabrina.

"I heard," said Isabel. She looked at me. "Congratulations." She turned to the rest of the group. "Clutterless Chloe, keeping things clean." Some of the kids laughed. Isabel had called me that before, in drama, but this time I heard how mean it was.

"Here's the thing, though," said Sabrina. "Someone stole Chloe's notebook during the fire drill. I mean, who does that?" I tugged on Sabrina's arm. She was making a mistake. Isabel wasn't in my class; she was in the class after mine. "Sabrina," I whispered.

Isabel's face became very still.

Sabrina ignored me and took a step closer to Isabel. "Would you know anything about that, Isabel?"

"Uh-oh," said one of the kids.

Isabel leaned over, unzipped her backpack, and tossed a notebook on the table. "You don't have to be so dramatic," she said.

"My notebook!" I leaned over and grabbed it. I tried not to hug it in front of the other kids.

"It was Laurel's idea, to get me the notebook. I was going to give it back," said Isabel sulkily. "I just wanted to look at it. With the fire drill, we have an extra day to get ready."

"You can't just take stuff that doesn't belong to you," I said, astonished. "That's, like, a rule from kindergarten."

Laurel lowered her head and mouthed, *Sorry*. But Isabel just shrugged. "So maybe it's a rule for babies."

"It's not!" A few other customers turned and looked at us. "It's a rule for people."

"Oh, I'm kidding," said Isabel coolly, though I doubted she meant it. "Look, my parents are really giving me a hard time about my grades. Laurel was only trying to help. I was just going to borrow your notebook, to use it as a reference. If I don't do well, my mom says I can't go on the Broadway trip."

Isabel leaned back in her chair. She was wearing a perfect white T-shirt with AMAZING written in tiny rhinestones across it, which matched her perfect white tennis shoes. Her nails were manicured into pink sparkly tips. She had everything, including, until recently, my notebook. She reached into her purse and tossed a couple of twenty-dollar bills on the table.

"Look," she said. "I'm happy to compensate you for your expertise. Sixty bucks for a couple of hours to look at your notebook. I know you need the money. I heard you say so."

For a hot second, I was tempted. Sixty dollars for something I had already done. Then my brain exploded. "No, that's not right," I said. "This is not something you get by throwing some money around." Sabrina tugged on my arm. I was shouting.

"It's not cheating," said Isabel. "I'll do my own work."

"You can't have it because you didn't ask," I said. "You can't just take stuff."

Henry's uncle appeared. "What's going on here? You girls are causing a disturbance."

Isabel flicked her hand. "It's nothing."

"She stole my notebook," I said forcefully. "I was getting it back."

Henry's uncle didn't seem to care about that. "You guys have a problem, you take it outside. The Tea Palace is a quiet place."

I took a quick peek around the restaurant, looking for Henry. If Henry were here, he'd be able to help me explain, tell his uncle that I had been wronged.

"If you ask your nephew, Henry . . ." I started.

"We're done," said Isabel, picking up the money and putting it away.

Oh, no we're not! declared my little voice. And this time we were in agreement.

"Not quite," I said. I picked up Isabel's drink—a strawberry slush with white boba—ripped off the seal, and dumped the drink over her head. The pink drink soaked her hair, dripped on her face, splotched her perfect white T-shirt.

"Chloe!" Sabrina gasped, and then put her hand over her mouth to keep from laughing. Isabel looked up at me in disbelief. A white boba pearl rolled over the top of her head and flew off, like a ski jumper.

"That's it," said Henry's uncle, pointing at me. "You are banned from Tea Palace!"

Auntie Sue

"I can't believe you did that!" exclaimed Sabrina. "I mean, Isabel totally deserved it, but I can't believe you did it." We were speed-walking away from Tea Palace. Everything was in a jumble. I was holding my drink, my backpack, my jacket, and my notebook, all in a messy pile. I had wanted to get out of there as quickly as possible, before Henry's uncle started yelling again.

"Neither can I." I felt like I had run a mile, though it was really my mind that was racing, not my heart. "Did I really just do that?" It felt like a dream.

"You did," said Sabrina. "Truth? It was kind of awesome." She wanted to high-five me, but I didn't have a free hand. Not that I felt like high-fiving.

"Do you think Isabel's parents are going to call my dad?"

"Maybe," Sabrina said. "But then you could point out that she stole your notebook, so maybe she'll just keep quiet."

"Mm-hmm." Suddenly, all I could think of was Henry, and how I wouldn't get to see him at Tea Palace anymore. *Don't be stupid. You can still see him at school.*

But why should I care about seeing him at all?

"I guess you'll have to get boba without me," I told Sabrina.

"No way!" said Sabrina. "I'm not going to patronize some place that banned my best friend!" She put her arm around me. "B-F-F-s before B-O-B-A. But talk to Henry. Maybe he can get you reinstated or something."

"I dunno. His uncle is kind of a hothead."

"Yeah, and hotheads are the least likely to stick to their guns because they know that they say a lot of dumb things when they're mad," said Sabrina. "Wait a few days and then see."

I felt so lucky to have a best friend like Sabrina. She was so loyal and smart and funny. I decided I should tell her the truth.

"There's a reason why I haven't signed up for the Broadway trip yet," I said. "And it's not because my dad said I had to raise the money. It's because . . ." I took a breath, trying to find the right words. "Things are different now."

Sabrina took my backpack and drink. "I know," she said softly. "How could it not be different?" She tipped her head so our foreheads were touching.

"Of course. I mean, what *isn't* different? But in this case, I mean money. It's tight. I don't want to stress my dad out by asking for money," I said. "And since my career as a baby-sitter has been cut short, I'm not sure what else I can do."

"I could ask my pare—" started Sabrina. I didn't let her finish.

"No way," I said firmly. "Look, this is the way it's going to be. My dad and I, we've got to figure it out."

"Oh . . . you're so stubborn," grumped Sabrina. "But I get it."

"You won't hate me if I can't go on the trip?" I asked.

"Oh, please," said Sabrina. "No way. But you still have time." Sabrina did not give up easily.

"Not much," I said. "Though now I guess I won't be spending my money on boba."

Sabrina suddenly stopped walking and laughed.

"What's so funny?" I asked.

"I was just thinking about Isabel," she said.

"And?"

"I've known you for five years," said Sabrina. "And I think this is the first time I've ever seen you make a mess on purpose!"

"There's always a first time for everything," I said. And then I had to laugh, too.

Auntie Sue showed up on Thursday after school, driving a new red convertible. She honked the horn and I went outside.

"Whoa!" I said. "Nice car!" I wasn't really a car person, not like some people I knew, but still. It looked like a fun car.

"Wait until you ride in it!" said Auntie Sue. "It's the best!" She jumped out of the car and hugged me. "We'll put down the top and hit the road!" Then I felt her stiffen and stand up. "Hello, Kurt."

Dad was standing on the front step, looking at us with his hands in his pockets. His usual smile was gone. He lifted one hand up in the air. "Hello, Sue. How are you?" he said formally.

"I'm fine. And you?" said Aunt Sue, just as formal.

I wished Aunt Sue and Dad would get along better. You would think that they could make each other happier with their shared memories of my mom. But instead, all they had were angry words at Mom's funeral. Auntie Sue scolded my dad for not stopping Mom from going to work; my dad said he couldn't make my mom stop. No one could. Because of the pandemic, Mom's funeral had been online, with squares of sad faces filling the screen. Mom felt responsible for the people who walked through the hospital no matter the reason. Dad and Auntie Sue only stopped fighting when I begged them to stop.

Auntie Sue and Dad made up, sort of, after that. Except they were always super polite with each other. But in a way, that was worse. They weren't using politeness to be kind. It was like it was what they used to keep from saying something terrible.

"I'll have Chloe home by bedtime," said Auntie Sue, rubbing my back. "Unless you want her sooner."

"Let's go with nine o'clock," said Dad. "It's a school night." He drooped a little, and I felt worried that Dad would feel lonely.

"It's Three Cup Chicken Thursday," I said. "Maybe we could . . ."

"Oh, uh . . . I don't really eat a lot of meat these days," said Auntie Sue.

"I need to finish off some leftovers," said Dad, defeating my plan. But just then, Phineas came hopping down the stairs.

"Who's this?" asked Auntie Sue. "You got a dog?" She knelt down and let Phineas smell her hand.

"He's here on a trial basis," I said. Phineas sat in front of Auntie Sue, a sure sign that he decided he liked her.

Auntie Sue didn't seem to hear me. "What a sweet face! What's his name?" She stroked the top of his head.

"Phineas," said Dad. "But Chloe isn't completely convinced."

Auntie Sue turned toward me, her mouth open in astonishment. "You don't want this dog?" She was acting like I said that I didn't want a million dollars.

"It's just that, well, dogs are messy. They get hair everywhere, and he messes up my homework. And I have to pick up his poo . . ."

"That's just part of having a dog!" protested Auntie Sue. "Look at that face. I'd love to get a dog, but I'm out of the house too much and it's just me." Out of the corner of my eye, I could see Dad nodding. Phineas looked at me and cocked his head to one side as if to say, *I'm pretty cute, aren't I?*

"He's getting fur all over your outfit!" I protested. Auntie Sue was wearing a tangerine jumpsuit, which was now accented with fur.

"Oh, that's not a big deal." Auntie Sue leaned down and brushed off the fur with her hands. "It's good to be clean, but not to the point of not doing things that are fun," said Auntie Sue.

"Well said," said Dad. I couldn't believe it. Dad and Auntie Sue actually agreed about something! Auntie Sue gave Phineas one last pat, and then Phineas went over and sat on Dad's foot.

"See? Your dad has company while we're out," said Auntie Sue. "Isn't that nice?"

The thought of Dad at least having Phineas for company

did make me feel a little better about leaving Dad at home. "Maybe you can think of something else for K-99 to train Phineas," I offered.

Dad nodded, not saying one way or the other what might happen. Then he waved as we got in the car and drove away.

11

Aunts, Uncles, and Other Disasters

Other girls might want to go clothes shopping or shoe shopping. But Auntie Sue knew exactly where I wanted to go.

The Neat Nook.

The Neat Nook was a store that specialized in selling organizing supplies, from spice racks for the kitchen to trays for jewelry to big hooks for hanging up bicycles in the garage. My favorite part was the section for office supplies—lots of sticky tabs and notebooks and pockets.

Auntie Sue lifted her hands and gestured to the entire store. "Whatever you want."

"Really?" I looked around the store, at all the neatly arranged boxes and other goodies, promising a perfectly arranged life.

"I owe you a birthday present, I'm pretty sure," said Auntie Sue. "And even if I didn't, it's my privilege as an auntie to spoil you."

The little voice in my head whispered, *You should ask Auntie Sue to help you with your Broadway trip.*

I tried to hush the little voice. *It's greedy to ask for something like that!*

No, it's not, the voice whispered back. *She said whatever you want! Did you see that car? She can afford it!*

My little voice and I could have kept arguing, but Auntie Sue called me over to the section for the bathroom. "I'm thinking of getting something for my makeup. What do you think?" she asked.

I pointed to a clear countertop organizer with compartments

for lipsticks. "I think that one is nice," I said. Auntie Sue always wore lipstick, even when she wasn't going out.

"Okay." She picked up the organizer and put it in a shopping basket. "You don't need to wear makeup! So young, so beautiful. I need to wear makeup. I'm old."

"You're not old!" I said. "And you always look pretty. Mom said you always had boys chasing after you."

"Ah! My favorite niece!" Auntie Sue put her arm around me and squeezed. She was loud enough that other people in the store turned around and looked at us. "It's true. I had a lot of suitors. Your mom would have, too, but she stuck to her studies."

"Did you ever want to marry any of your boyfriends?" I asked.

"There was one, but . . ." She shrugged. "It didn't work out." She walked a few steps away and pointed to a shelf that went under the bathroom sink. Then she lowered her voice and said, "Ni dà yí mā lái le ma?"

I was confused. Auntie Sue was my yí mā, or aunt. Dà yí

mā meant great-aunt. Either way, I wasn't sure why she was asking if my great-aunt was here!

Auntie Sue could see I didn't quite get it. She shook her head and pointed to a box of Tampax on the display. "Ni dà yí mā lái le ma?" she repeated, more slowly.

Has your great aunt arrived? Why would she ask that? Then my brain clicked. "Oh! You mean Aunt Flo?"

Now it was Auntie Sue's turn to be confused. "Who is Aunt Flo?"

"That's what some people call getting your period," I said. "They say Aunt Flo is visiting."

Auntie Sue burst out laughing. "And I was taught to say, 'My great-aunt is coming!'" That was so funny, both languages talking about aunts! Maybe it was a sign. Maybe I should ask her about the trip.

When we both stopped laughing, I told her that I hadn't gotten my period yet. Asking about money for the trip was on the tip of my tongue when Auntie Sue said, "When it happens, you call me. Your dad won't know what to do."

"I know what to do," I said. "We learned in health class." Plus, Sabrina had also already gotten her period.

"But you'll want to tell someone," Aunt Sue insisted. "You should tell someone. You can tell me."

"Okay," I said. "I mean, I'll tell Dad, but I can tell you, too."

"Don't tell your dad! He's a man!" said Auntie Sue.

I didn't like the feeling that Auntie Sue was implying that I couldn't talk to Dad about something. "He's my dad," I said. "He should know. He'll have to buy me stuff."

Auntie Sue covered her face with her hands. "I can send it to you. I can set up a monthly delivery."

"I'll be fine," I said. I was trying to be nice about it, but part of me felt upset. I was going to say *I can talk to my dad about anything*, but then I remembered the trip to Broadway. Still, my dad was a good dad, and I didn't like Auntie Sue trying to control what we talked about. Now I was glad I hadn't said anything about the Broadway trip. I picked out a few things for school—some sticker tabs and a tiny vacuum for sucking up eraser bits. Auntie Sue seemed to sense that something had changed. After she paid for our things, she turned to me, put on an extra-big smile, and said, "Let's go get some boba now!"

Things were going from bad to worse. I took the bag from the cashier. "No," I said. "It's okay."

"Come on! Don't be like that. Don't you like boba?"

Did I like boba? What wasn't to like about taro and Thai tea and all the other amazing flavors?

And Henry, my little voice added.

Hush, I told my little voice. *But he's not that bad*, I added.

Auntie Sue peered into my face. "You told me you liked boba," she said. "And I looked it up. Tea Palace, right?"

"The thing is . . ." I said slowly. This was so embarrassing. "I've been banned from Tea Palace." Now it was my turn to whisper.

Auntie Sue's eyebrows sprang up into two high arches. "Banned? You? How is that possible?" Her indignation on my behalf made me feel warm toward her again. Auntie Sue did love me, even if she got carried away sometimes.

If I thought Auntie Sue was mad before, she was *really* mad after I told her the whole story in the car. She was mad at Laurel for stealing my notebook, Isabel for being a jerk, the other kids who just sat there, and Henry's uncle at Tea Palace. "He should have defended you!" she said. "What happened to sticking up for what's right?"

"He didn't like that we were causing a commotion," I said. "And then I really added to the commotion."

"Humph," said Auntie Sue. She sped up a little, and the buzz from the car engine grew louder. "We're going over there right now, and I am going to *straighten this out*. Some things are more important than making a commotion!"

Auntie Sue found a parking spot right by the front. She charged through the front door and stood with her hands on her hips, like one of those gunslingers in the Old West movies, about to challenge someone to a duel.

"May I help you?" called one of the girls from the counter.

I took a quick peek and did not see Henry. I wasn't sure if that was a good thing or a bad thing.

"I'd like to speak to the head of this establishment," said Auntie Sue.

"Oh, you must mean Martin," said the girl. "He's over by the bridge, trying to fix the stream. The pump is broken or something."

I showed Auntie Sue where the bridge was. Sure enough, a man was lying on the floor, with his head under the bridge. Henry was there, too, handing him tools.

"Chloe!" said Henry. His face brightened. "What are you doing here?"

"My aunt wants to talk to your uncle," I said. Auntie Sue had taken a step closer to the bridge and was tapping her foot near the man.

Henry leaned down and shook the man's arm. "Dà jiù, a customer wants to talk to you," he said.

"Děng yīxià. I've almost gotten this bridge fixed," said his uncle. His face was hidden by the bridge, but he sounded irritated.

"It's urgent," said Auntie Sue loudly. "It's about my niece, who you banned from your establishment."

The man started to sit up, then smacked his head on the bridge. He let out a loud angry groan. This did not seem a good way to get me reinstated at Tea Palace. The man slid forward a few inches and sat up, this time clearing the bridge.

"Your niece," said Henry's uncle, rubbing the spot on his head where he'd banged it under the bridge, "was caus-ing quite a disturbance . . ." He stopped talking and took a closer look at Auntie Sue.

"Your niece!" he exclaimed. "Your niece!" Maybe he had gotten a concussion. He kept repeating the same words as he gazed, open-mouthed, at us.

Then he added. "Sue?" He got slowly to his feet and leaned in closer.

"Wait . . . you guys know each other?" said Henry. Which was exactly what I was thinking.

Auntie Sue had gone from righteous anger to total shock. "Martin?" she said.

"Yes. Me. Martin," said Henry's uncle. They just stood there, looking at each other. Then he pulled out a chair, sat down, and gestured to another chair. "Sit, sit."

Auntie Sue stayed standing. Her mouth was trembling.

"Sue Tseng. After all these years," said Henry's uncle, not noticing that Auntie Sue had not responded yet. "How can this be happening?" He almost started smiling, which was an expression I'd never seen before. "And this is your niece! That changes everything."

I guessed that meant I was reinstated. Except Auntie Sue was still silent. "Are you okay?" I asked Auntie Sue.

She shook her head as if she were waking up from a dream. Then she reached over, grabbed my hand, and began pulling me toward the door. "Let's go," she said.

"Sue! Wait!" said Henry's uncle. Auntie Sue did not respond.

As Auntie Sue dragged me toward the door, I turned back to look at Henry. He looked just as confused as I felt. I shook my head to show him that I didn't know what was going on.

Running Away

Auntie Sue didn't say anything. She just started driving, away from Tea Palace, away from the direction of the house.

"Do you know where we're going?" I asked. She didn't answer.

"My house is in the other direction," I said. She still didn't say anything. She just stared out the windshield and kept driving. The hum of the motor was the only sound in the car. I tried to imagine what would make Auntie Sue behave like that. My loud, opinionated aunt had practically turned to stone.

She started driving faster, zipping through traffic lights right before they turned red, past other cars. She was running away in the car and taking me with her. Finally, I said, "Auntie Sue, you're scaring me. Can you pull over, please?" When I said that, she swung into an empty school parking lot and shut off the motor abruptly.

I reached over and touched her arm. "What's going on? Why are you acting like this?"

Auntie Sue took a deep breath. "I was feeling a little upset."

"Yeah. I could tell *that*." I waited, not asking the question I wanted to ask. *What made you act like that?* But Auntie Sue answered it.

"That man in the Tea Palace. Martin Chang." Her voice shook when she said his name. "I have not seen him since I was twenty."

I unbuckled my seat belt so I could see Auntie Sue better.

"Wait, wait. Back up. You knew that guy. How did you know him?"

"We met in a bookstore," said Auntie Sue. "I had gotten Amy Tan's memoir, and we started talking about her books. *The Joy Luck Club. The Hundred Secret Senses.* The bookstore trip turned into coffee. Coffee turned into dinner. We couldn't stop talking to each other." She stopped, staring into the air. "He was so funny! He made me laugh."

I couldn't imagine Henry's uncle making anyone laugh, but I went with it. "So, wait—if he was so great, why did you act like that when you saw him?"

"We had this amazing, whirlwind month. We loved doing the same things. We went to the movies and the museum. We tried new restaurants. And then"—she snapped her fingers—"he disappeared."

"What?!" I exclaimed. "Maybe his phone died."

"He didn't return my calls, my emails. Social media wasn't really a thing in those days."

"So you thought he was dead," I said.

"Did I think he was actually dead? I checked the newspapers, the police blotters, but didn't find anything about him. But at some point, I had to go on with my life. I told myself he was dead so I would stop torturing myself." She rubbed her hands over the steering wheel, making a circle. "Remember when you asked me if I wanted to marry any of my boyfriends? He was the one."

"But then you should be excited to see him," I said, confused.

She shook her head. "Obviously, he didn't feel the same way about me." She looked out the window and blinked. "What kind of person just disappears like that? Someone who doesn't care about the other person. Wants to escape them."

"It could be something else," I said.

"Like what?"

"I don't know. Maybe you're right," I said reluctantly. This was one of the scary things about love. You never knew when it might turn on you, make you sad, break your heart.

A shiny popping boba one minute, and then squish—it was gone.

Auntie Sue started laughing a little hysterically. "I guess you won't be getting boba today." She coughed and straightened up. "I'm sorry about that."

"It's okay," I said. "I kind of forgot about that part, about getting boba." It was hard to imagine Auntie Sue being so head over heels in love. She was always so driven, always doing something. By herself. I thought she had gotten too old to care about being with someone, but now I wasn't sure.

"You can't go back there," said Auntie Sue, sounding more like her old self. "The way that man treated me. It's just not acceptable. It would be like saying the way he treated me was okay."

"Well . . ." I stalled. I did want to go back to Tea Palace. But maybe family loyalty was more important?

"He disrespected me," said Auntie Sue. "That's not how you treat someone."

I didn't know what to say, but it felt like I had to say some-thing. "You're right."

"But I know what you're thinking," said Auntie Sue.

"You do?"

"You're wondering how you'll get boba if you can't go to the Tea Palace," said Auntie Sue confidently.

That was not what I was thinking, but it was a reason-able question. "Is there another way to get boba?" I asked. "Around here?"

Auntie Sue started the car engine. "Leave it to me," she said. "We just need to stop by a few stores."

We went to the Asian grocery store, where Auntie Sue filled up the cart. She found things I didn't even know the store had, like a big bag of boba. When we came home, Dad looked surprised.

"I thought you guys were going to be out longer," he said. "And what is this?" I could see why Dad was confused. The boba looked like a sack of vacuum-packed marbles.

"That's boba," said Auntie Sue. "Chloe and I have decided that she's better off making boba at home."

We had also gotten bags of frozen fruit, plus cans of condensed milk. Auntie Sue had also wanted to buy some black tea, but I told her that we had some at home.

"This is a lot of stuff for one drink," said Dad, rubbing the back of his neck.

"This is for more than one drink," I explained. "Auntie Sue wanted me to stock up so I can make my own boba drinks anytime."

Dad smiled. "That's very generous of you, Sue."

"I don't think Chloe should be going to Tea Palace," said Auntie Sue. Dad looked over at me, mystified. I mouthed, *Old boyfriend.* Dad nodded and pressed his lips together. I had to give Dad credit for knowing when to keep quiet. Phineas curled up in a circle and let out a yawn.

"What did you do to him?" I teased Dad. "He's so sleepy." I rubbed Phinny behind the ears.

"Well, actually," said Dad. "While you guys were out,

some people came by to meet him. They're looking for a dog to adopt. They ended up taking him for a walk and playing with him for a long time."

"Oh." I sat down on the floor, next to Phinny. He pushed his nose into my hand, and I petted him. "So, we're not keeping him?"

"I mean, you were the one who said you wanted a trial period, and it seems like you don't really like him." Dad sighed. "After the whole notebook thing . . . but you could change your mind."

I didn't know what to say. Did I want Phineas, with all of his messes and slobber? Or did I want to go back to the way things were?

Phineas poked his head up, alert to a noise outside. Then someone knocked on the door.

"Are you expecting anyone?" asked Dad. Dad had posted a sign that said NO SOLICITORS, but people knocked on the door anyway, trying to sell things. I shook my head. Phineas let out a loud bark.

Dad opened the door partway. "May I help you?" he asked.

"Is this, um, Chloe Wong's house?" said a voice. I peeked around the door. It was Henry!

When Henry saw me, he let out a sigh of relief. "Oh good. I was kind of terrified I had the wrong house. Sabrina couldn't remember the house number, so I had to guess based on her description."

"What are you doing here?" I asked. *His uncle sent him here to banish you from Tea Palace again*, suggested the little voice in my head.

"It's not, um, me, exactly. It's my uncle Martin." Henry pointed toward the road. A man stood on the sidewalk, with his hands clasped together and shoulders hunched. Uncle Martin didn't look like the scary guy in the café at all now. He just looked sad.

"My uncle wants to talk to your aunt," said Henry.

"What's going on?" Dad hadn't moved from his place behind the door. Phineas whined. He wanted to go outside and meet the new people.

"This is Auntie Sue's old boyfriend," I whispered.

"Oh boy," said Dad. He stepped back so he was no longer between Auntie Sue and the door.

"Do you want to talk to him?" I asked Auntie Sue. Auntie Sue had pressed herself against the closet door, out of sight.

"Do *you* think I should talk to him?" asked Auntie Sue.

"Why are you asking me?" I said. "I've never had a boyfriend."

"He's your friend's uncle," argued Auntie Sue.

"It seems kind of rude to leave him standing out there." I peeked again. I supposed that, technically, he wasn't standing. Henry had rejoined his uncle, and they were walking in little circles in our front yard.

"I'm the rude one? He disappeared," retorted Auntie Sue in a fierce whisper. She made a hissing sound when she said *disappeared*.

"But you said he must not have liked you. If he's here, it seems like that's not the case," I whispered back.

"Maybe he feels guilty," said Auntie Sue.

"Maybe," I said.

"But only because he's been caught," she added. "He could have found me."

"Maybe he has an explanation of where he's been," I offered.

"Humph." But she looked tempted. And scared. She crossed her arms and then uncrossed them. She chewed on her thumbnail.

"Maybe the best way to find out is to go talk to him," I said. I couldn't believe Auntie Sue was acting like this. She was normally so decisive.

"Is someone coming out?" asked Henry.

"Just a second," I called. I looked at Auntie Sue and gestured to the door.

Auntie Sue didn't say anything for a moment, bowing her head low. Then she tossed her head up, pulled her shoulders back, and strode toward the door. "I'll give him five minutes," she said.

Is this what love did to people? Made them act desperate

and angry, sad and confused? And how did you clean up a mess like that?

Phineas pawed at the door, wanting to join the people outside. From the doorway, I could see Auntie Sue's back, shoulders square and arms folded. Uncle Martin was talking, but I couldn't hear what he was saying.

Phineas barked and whined. I reached down to grab his collar at the same time Phinny got up on his hind legs and pushed against the door. The door swung open, and Phinny ran outside, sprinting toward Auntie Sue and Henry's uncle, standing near the curb. From the corner of my eye, I saw a truck turn around the corner.

If Phinny ran into the street . . .

"No!" I ran after Phineas, but he was too fast for me. He wasn't slowing down. He was going to run into the street.

"Grab him!" I shouted. Everything seemed to be happening in slow motion. Auntie Sue turned toward me, mouth open, not quite seeing what was happening. "The dog!"

"Chloe! Phineas!" Dad was shouting behind me. No one

was close enough to Phineas. The truck brakes groaned and squealed.

Suddenly, a figure dashed out and tackled Phineas to the curb. Henry. "Gotcha!" Their heads were hung over the curb, into the street. The truck driver looked at us, mouth slightly open. He shook his head and then kept driving.

"It's okay, Chloe. It's okay." It was Dad. "See? Phinny is okay. Don't cry." I didn't realize I was crying.

"He could have been hit. Or killed," I said, trying to sound normal while taking huge gulps of air. I didn't want Henry to see me cry.

"He didn't. Thanks to, um, this guy." Dad gestured awkwardly toward Henry.

"Henry." Henry and I said his name at the same time.

Auntie Sue and Henry's uncle came over, their faces pale. "Is everything okay? Is Chloe okay?" Auntie Sue said.

Was I okay? Why was everyone talking about me? It was Phineas who had almost been hit by a truck. I could still smell the exhaust. Phineas looked up at me, doing the panting smile he always did.

"Thank you," said Dad to Henry. "That was really brave." Henry nodded and then turned away, blushing.

It was too much, this tangle of feelings. Feeling afraid, feeling uncertain. Seeing Henry's uncle and Auntie Sue together, wondering if they were happy or sad. And then being grateful for Henry.

"Do you want him?" I asked suddenly. Henry's eyes widened, surprised.

"Who? The dog?" he asked.

No, You're Immature

"You said WHAT?" exclaimed Sabrina at lunch.

"I asked Henry if he wanted Phineas," I said uncomfortably. "I just think that, um, he's too much dog for just me and my dad. Anyway, Henry said no."

"Of course he did," said Sabrina. "Because offering to give away your dog just because he got away from you is a terrible idea. You don't mean it."

"I did," I said stubbornly. "He's too much work. It's like trying to organize a bowl of spaghetti, keeping up with that dog." I didn't tell Sabrina how sick it made me, in those few seconds, to think about losing Phineas. It was too scary, too overwhelming. It would be better to just let him go.

"You and your constant desire for neatness," said Sabrina. "Honestly." We both didn't say anything for a moment. Sabrina and I usually did not fight, so I wasn't sure what to do next. Sabrina changed the subject.

"So what happened to Auntie Sue and Henry's uncle then?" asked Sabrina. "Did they kiss and make up?"

"I didn't see anything," I confessed. "I took Phineas inside, and then we just sat on the couch for a while."

"So upset about the dog that *you don't want*," said Sabrina, poking me.

"My dad came inside and said that Auntie Sue had to go, and that she'd get in touch later," I told her.

"That's it?" asked Sabrina. "So why didn't you ask her what happened? I would have been like, *Lady, you need to spill some tea, now.*"

"That seems a little personal," I said.

"A little personal?! It was like a whole soap opera in your front yard."

"She'll tell me when she's ready," I said.

Sabrina. She puffed up her cheeks and then blew out a whoosh of air. Then she spotted Henry walking across the cafeteria, carrying a tray. "Maybe Henry knows. Henry! Hey, Henry!"

"You don't have to . . ." I started to say. But Henry had heard Sabrina and made his way over.

"Hey, guys, what's up?" he asked.

"What's up? What's going on with your uncle and Chloe's aunt? It's unbelievable that they knew each other before," said Sabrina.

"I know, right? I was so confused when Chloe came in with this totally demanding woman, and then it turns out my uncle knew her," said Henry.

"My aunt wasn't being demanding!" I said. "She was defending me."

"She came in kind of hot," said Henry to Sabrina, ignoring

me. "My uncle was in the middle of fixing the stream in the restaurant, and she stood over him and just started yelling at him."

"Your uncle was the one who just up and disappeared after they started dating," I pointed out. Henry didn't have an answer to that.

"Okay," said Sabrina. "But your uncle obviously wanted to talk to Aunt Sue. That's why you went to Chloe's house. What happened when they talked?"

"I dunno," said Henry. "I left after I rescued the dog."

"You *left*?" said Sabrina, astounded.

"I had to get back to work at Tea Palace," Henry explained. "Also, it was kind of not my business."

Sabrina looked at both of us, open-mouthed. "What is it with you two? Of course it's your business! It was kind of your business when your uncle asked you to take him to Chloe's house," argued Sabrina. She turned to me. "And it was kind of your business when your aunt got you re-banished from Tea Palace!"

Henry shrugged. "He asked me to help him find that lady," he said as if that was enough explanation.

"What did your uncle say when he came back?" I asked.

"What did your aunt say when *she* came back?" countered Henry.

"I asked first," I said.

"This whole thing started because your aunt showed up at my uncle's place of business," said Henry.

"No, it started way before that. Like, when they were practically teenagers," I said.

"So it shouldn't be a big deal, whatever she had to say," said Henry.

"My aunt had to leave. She had work to do," I said. It was like we were spies, trying to outsmart each other for information on the other side.

"My uncle had to get back to Tea Palace to repair the stream," said Henry. "Since he was so rudely interrupted."

Henry and I stopped talking and sized each other up.

Henry's dimple was threatening to emerge. Was he laughing at me?

"I see you've managed to get boba from somewhere," said Henry. "Though it's not Tea Palace." He nodded at the jar in my hand. "Where'd you get it?"

"Wouldn't you like to know!" I said. Henry was holding out on me, not sharing important information, so it felt okay to hold some information from him.

Henry narrowed his eyes at me. "Seriously, where'd you get it?"

"I'll tell you when you tell me what your uncle said," I said. I meant to say it in a teasing way, but it came out a little harsh. Also, I didn't like the way Henry was talking.

"Did another boba place open up?" asked Henry.

"Maybe, maybe not," I said. I took an extra-long sip and waved the glass around. I was going to tell Henry that I had made it, but he scowled at me.

"You're so immature," said Henry. Then he walked away

without saying another word. When he did that, I felt sick. And mad. I wanted to say, *No, you're immature*, but that seemed kind of immature in itself. Then to make things worse, he stopped at Isabel Zhang's table and said something, and the whole table laughed. Were they laughing at me? Isabel and I had not spoken since the Tea Palace incident, though we occasionally gave each other dirty looks. I'd heard Isabel had gotten a D on her notebook, but her parents were letting her go on the trip anyway. According to the board, there were seven slots left, which did not feel lucky.

Sabrina leaned over and helped herself to a sip of my drink. "This boba is really good," said Sabrina as if nothing was happening.

"I can't believe he just said that," I said. Me, immature? No one had ever said that to me. I also couldn't believe he was talking to Isabel after what she had done to me!

"Aw, he'll get over it," said Sabrina.

"He might; I might not," I said.

"Then you guys will be like your aunt and his uncle," said Sabrina, wiggling her eyebrows.

"Knock it off!" I said. "We're nothing like them." But what did that mean? Because we did or did not get along?

"He's just mad that you have boba and it's not from Tea Palace. Where did you get it, anyway? With the mason jar? So cool."

"I made it at home," I said. "My aunt helped me get the ingredients from the Asian grocery store. Look! Mason jars come with these flat canning lids that fit inside the ring. I punched a hole in the lid so a straw could fit, but still keep the drink from splashing out."

"Ooh! Nice! Very clever. You need to bring me one," said Sabrina. "Since I am banning myself from Tea Palace in solidarity with you."

"I'll bring you one tomorrow," I promised. I tried to focus on that rather than the sting of Henry calling me *immature* and then walking away. "What Henry do you want?"

"What'd you say?" Luckily, I had spoken while Sabrina was taking a noisy slurp.

Oooh, why did I say that? "What *flavor* boba do you want? Do you want strawberry?" Focus, Chloe! Do not think about stupid Henry.

Carly was walking by with her friends and overheard us. "Are you taking orders?" she called. "That looks really good." She came closer and picked up the jar. "And I love that it's eco-friendly. I always feel a little guilty about the plastic. Who's doing this?"

Sabrina put her arm around me. "Oh, it's a new store, really exclusive for now. But we can get you an order."

"Maybe you could bring it to the soccer game after school tomorrow?" asked Carly. Our school had an intramural soccer league. Carly's friend Jenna poked her. "Don't leave us out."

"You can bring drinks for all of us, right?" asked Carly. There were six of them.

"Ummm . . ." I started. "The thing is . . ."

"They're five dollars each," said Sabrina brightly. "Tell your friends. We might be able to get some extras."

"Not too many friends," I said nervously.

"Don't forget your money!" said Sabrina.

Big Boba

I waited until Carly and her friends had walked away before getting into it with Sabrina. "What are you doing? This is just for us! I'm not a boba shop."

"But why not?" said Sabrina. "As my mom says, it's as easy to cook for twenty as it is for one. It's just a question of volume."

"Why not? Um, let's see. I don't know if I have enough ingredients. I definitely don't have enough jars. And how

am I going to get a bunch of boba drinks to a soccer game?"
I complained.

"Eh. Minor detail," said Sabrina calmly.

"It's not minor!" I squawked. "What am I supposed to do?
Go buy mason jars? I don't have that kind of money!" I didn't
know how much mason jars cost.

"I'm not asking you to buy, I don't know, gold blocks,"
said Sabrina. "I bet you have enough to buy a dozen. Check
around your house, too. Everyone goes through an *I'm going
to make my own jelly* phase at least once."

"And then, what, grow multiple hands to carry all these
jars?" Clearly, Sabrina had not thought this through. I could
carry one jar in each hand, but more than that was impossible. I did not like this feeling. This feeling of spontaneous
activities without a thought-out plan. "You're used to your
family's restaurant. I'm not a restaurant! There's no way I
can get more than two jars there."

"Actually," said Sabrina. "I was thinking of that red

wagon that we used to play with when we were little, pretending that the puller was a horse."

I knew the wagon she was talking about—it was in the shed. My mom had used it to haul around her gardening supplies when I had outgrown it. She grew strawberries and blueberries and tomatoes in the summer. But the wagon only made Sabrina's idea seem only slightly less impossible.

"You're gonna do this," said Sabrina. "And make enough money for Broadway. There are only seven slots left, but you can make enough money if we hurry."

Ohhhhh. *Money for Broadway.* That's why my best friend was trying to stress me out. "That's, like, seventy or eighty drinks, plus costs for jars and stuff," I said. "How can I possibly make that much?"

Sabrina rolled her eyes. "Just multiply—it's not that hard. If you can make one, you can make forty. You've got this." She corrected herself. "*We've* got this. Got any more obstacles for me to solve?" She was grinning. And I had to admit, she was right. I just had to recalculate the recipe I was using.

"How do I keep from strangling my friend who makes up these schemes for me?" I asked. I put my arm around her and squeezed. Suddenly, the trip felt possible again.

"Ohhh, I don't have the answer for that," said Sabrina. "I guess you'll have to keep putting up with me."

Every boba drink has some basic parts—ice, tea, milk, and add-ins. What changes is the flavor of the tea, and the combination of boba or toppings. The first thing Sabrina and I had to decide was what flavor tea to have. We couldn't have them all—that was too complicated. Sabrina came over to my house with a big pot from her family's restaurants. She also had mason jars.

"Found 'em in the storage room," said Sabrina. "Never know what you'll find back there." She rubbed her hands together. "Now what's the game plan?"

"I think I'll make strawberry milk tea," I suggested. "I'll just need to make more strawberry milk to add to the black tea. That's pretty easy." Phineas looked at us and whined. He wanted attention. I leaned over and rubbed him with my foot so my hands would stay clean. Sabrina watched us.

"You're so much nicer to Phineas now that you say you're giving him away," she said.

"No, I'm not," I said. "I've always been nice to Phinny."

"So why let him go?"

"Will you drop it?" I said. I thought that making the decision to let Phinny go would make me feel calmer, but it didn't. "Let's focus on the boba. What do you think should be the second flavor?"

"Mmmm . . . what's that one that Henry gave you?"

"I don't remember," I lied. "It wasn't that good."

"The purple drink? You didn't like it? You acted like you did," said Sabrina. Sabrina looked genuinely confused.

Why was I lying to my best friend? "Oh yeah. I was, uh, thinking of something else. It was, uh, taro. Taro is good." I got up and opened the freezer door. "I think we have some in the freezer from when Dad makes taro cakes." I actually already knew we had frozen taro root. I just wanted to cool off my burning face. "Yup, we have some."

"Awesome! And here's a recipe for taro milk tea online," said Sabrina.

"Let's get started, and then, while everything is cooking, we can look for more jars," I said. The taro would have to be cooked in hot water for a while, and we also had to make tea. A lot of tea.

After we got everything set up on the stove, we went down to my dad's workshop to ask if he knew if we had any more mason jars. Phineas followed us. Dad was tinkering with a new feature for K-99, a ball thrower. "Fetch! Good dog! Fetch!" droned the robot. A metal arm with a scoop on the end clicked back and then sprung forward.

"New feature, huh?" I asked Dad.

"It works fine," said Dad. "But Phinny doesn't seem as

interested in playing fetch with K-99 as he is with us. I'm trying to figure out how to make the robot sound more like us."

I asked Dad if he knew whether we had any mason jars, and Dad pointed to a corner of the basement. Phineas found a tennis ball and brought it to me. "Not now, Phinny," I said. "We can play later, after we find the mason jars." Phineas dropped the ball, sighed, and wandered away.

One box was filled with papers. And then one had dinner plates, each one wrapped in newspaper. Each plate had a frilly gold design on it. "I don't remember these plates at all."

"My mom says that she and my dad registered for all sorts of fancy stuff when they were getting married," said Sabrina. "Now they never use them."

Phineas nudged my hand and tried to give me a baseball hat. "Where did you get that?" I asked him. I put the hat on his big furry head, and Phinny sat down, looking very pleased with himself.

"He's a handsome boy," said Sabrina. She reached over and rubbed his neck. "Such a good boy." Phinny closed his eyes, enjoying the attention.

I rewrapped the plate, put it away, and then tugged on another box. Two packs of mason jars, still wrapped in plastic! "Bingo," I said. "Looks like there are two dozen."

"Great!" said Sabrina. "With the ones from the restaurant, we should have plenty. We need to wash them out, though. Customers will want to know your stuff is clean."

"We can run them through the dishwasher," I said. But I was more interested in the index card I found tucked in the side of the box. It was a recipe for blueberry-lemon jam, written in my mom's handwriting. "Look!"

Mom believed in writing things by hand. She said you remembered things better that way. The letters looped across the card. Eight cups fresh blueberries. Pectin. Juice and zest of two lemons. I held the card up to my face and sniffed, hoping it would smell like Mom, but it just smelled like regular paper.

"That looks like your handwriting," said Sabrina.

"It's my mom's," I told her. "I guess she was going to make this, but she never got to."

"She makes z's the same way you do," said Sabrina, pointing to the z in *zest*. The z made a bump and then looped below the bottom line.

"That's funny," I said. "I wasn't even trying. At least I don't think." My chest felt warm and glowy. Mom was still with me, in a way I hadn't expected.

"It's better that way," said Sabrina. "Don't you think? It's like you're like her without thinking. Like, genetics."

"You definitely have her smile," said Dad. Everyone says I look like my dad, so this was something I wasn't used to hearing. "Her beautiful smile." When Dad said that, he and Sabrina both stared right at my mouth, which made me feel weird. And smile. Like my mom.

"I feel like we should have one more thing," I said, mostly to change the subject. "It doesn't feel like a genuine boba tea business yet."

"I wish we could sell popping boba," said Sabrina. "I don't suppose they sell that at the Asian grocery."

"I didn't see any," I said. Though the shelves had been crammed full of things I hadn't noticed before.

"You can make popping boba," said Dad. He started looking through the shelves of his workshop, moving things as he talked. "It's a fairly simple spherification process."

"A what-if-cation process?" said Sabrina.

"Spherification," said Dad. "Sphere, you know, like a ball? That's what those popping boba are. Basically it's a very thin gel wall wrapped around a ball of liquid."

"Wait, how do you know about this?" I asked. "I didn't think you were into boba tea."

"I'm not into boba tea, but I know it's popular. Especially with you guys," said Dad casually. "And there was an article about it in *Popular Science*." He held up a bottle marked CALCIUM LACTATE. "We just need to find some sodium alginate, and we're in business."

"Oh, sure," said Sabrina. "Everyone definitely has that lying around." She was being sarcastic, but Dad didn't seem to pick up on that.

"If you have acid reflux, you should," said Dad. "The alginate makes a barrier to keep the acid from coming up. That same tendency is what helps make the wall of the popping boba. Did you know it's made from seaweed?" Dad opened up a cabinet and pulled out a bag. "Bingo."

Dad showed us how to make the popping boba in the kitchen, which turned out to be easier than I thought it would be. We added two teaspoons of calcium lactate to two cups of water in a casserole dish and stirred until the powder disappeared. Then Dad said we should pick a flavor of juice and add sodium alginate to it. I poked around the pantry and found a bottle of peach juice.

"Perfect!" said Sabrina. "That will go with strawberry and taro. Plus, I've never had peach popping boba."

Dad had us mix just a tiny bit of sodium alginate to the

juice. We had to measure and figure out what 1 percent of sodium alginate would be.

"Math!" cried Sabrina. "It's a trick to make us do math."

"Says the person who said I just had to multiply to make a bigger batch of boba," I said, giving her a nudge.

"It's different when *I* have to do it," said Sabrina.

"Math can be yummy," said Dad.

"They should make math yummy more often," I said. "Then fewer people would complain about it." Phineas brought me the tennis ball again, wagging his tail hopefully. "I'm cooking now, Phinny. Later, okay? I promise."

We mixed up the juice and sodium alginate in the blender and then waited for the bubbles to disappear. Once all the bubbles were gone, Dad filled an eyedropper with juice and had us put drops of the peach mixture in the casserole dish. "Watch."

A pale orange drop landed in the clear liquid—and then stayed that way!

"It's not spreading out," said Sabrina.

"The reaction between the sodium alginate and the calcium lactate makes a skin," said Dad. "A wall that wraps up the liquid." He kept making drops. Five more perfect balls appeared in the liquid, and Dad handed the eyedropper to Sabrina. "Now you try it."

A stream of liquid squirted into the water and became a worm. "Oh no! I squeezed it too hard," said Sabrina.

"It all tastes the same," said Dad. "No matter what shape they are."

"And it shows that this is all handmade," I said. Sabrina made a few more. This time they were round.

"You can scoop out the popping boba with a mesh strainer and then make more," said Dad. "Give 'em a little rinse under water."

I made some, and then Sabrina made more. We scooped them out, rinsed them, and put them in a bowl. "Let's try one," I said. We each used our fingers like tweezers and took one. Sabrina picked the wormy one. I gave one to Dad.

I'd never paid such careful attention to a popping boba,

how it felt in my mouth, or how much I had to press down to make it pop. I guess it's different when you make it yourself. The sweet peachy liquid spread over my tongue.

"It's good!" said Sabrina.

"It's really good," I said. I had thought maybe it wouldn't taste as good as the ones we got in the store, but they tasted the same, maybe even better. "I just hope we don't eat them all before we get to the game tomorrow!"

"You'll have the money—" started Sabrina. I realized that she was about to say *for Broadway,* because she thought Dad knew about the trip.

I picked up the ball Phineas had left for me and shouted, "Phineas, FETCH!" as loudly as I could while throwing the ball at the door. The ball thumped on the door, making Phinny think someone was knocking. He started barking.

"What on earth!" said Dad. He got up to check the door. Sabrina gave me a weird look.

"What was that all about?" she asked.

I shrugged. "Phineas wanted to play fetch," I said.

"First Isabel, now Phinny," said Sabrina. "Are you really Chloe? Who is this person causing all this . . . confusion?"

"Maybe I've changed. Now I'm Chaotic Chloe," I said.

"Likely story!" said Sabrina, pointing at the table. I had started lining up the popping boba into neat rows.

"I still haven't told my dad about the trip," I admitted.

"What?" said Sabrina. "You're going to have to tell him. We're going to make the money!"

"We might," I said.

"We will," said Sabrina. "And you better be ready to go when we do!"

15

Messy Methods to Make Money

It turned out we were just getting started when we made all the components of boba. There was so much to think about—making sure we had enough supplies, how to keep the ice cold. Plus, if part of our plan was to use glass jars, we had to have a way of getting them back.

"We could give people a quarter for bringing them back," I suggested. "That's what they do at the airport to get people to bring back the cart. Isn't it, Phinny?" Phineas was hanging out in the kitchen with us. We had to keep stepping over him because he took up so much space. Phinny let out a low, grumbly sigh.

"Maybe," said Sabrina. She put on her jacket, getting ready to go. "I might have an idea. Come here, Phinny." Phinny padded over to her, and Sabrina gave him a big hug around the neck and around the middle. "What a good boy," she said. "What a good, good boy."

"You're being weird," I said.

"Gotta get my hugs in while I can," said Sabrina. She gave me a long look. "You should, too."

The next day after school, Sabrina came over to my house, so we could load up the wagon, and then take it back to school. The jars rattled and clinked over every crack in the sidewalk. Plus, I brought Phineas. "He needs to get out," I told Sabrina.

"He'll be a great way to draw attention," said Sabrina. She was right. As soon as we arrived, kids started crowding around the wagon, asking for drinks and petting

Phinny. He soaked up the attention, closing his eyes and smiling.

"Please form a line," I said. I didn't like the feeling of being jostled, of people pressing in. No one seemed to hear me. "We'll take care of everyone in turn." Phineas opened his eyes and added a loud *Woof!* When he did that, a line quickly formed.

"Thank you, Phineas," I said.

Sabrina turned to me and smiled. "Ready to open?" I nodded.

"Oops, one last detail." Sabrina reached into her bag and pulled out a jar marked TIPS. Sabrina really did think of everything. Then she gestured to the first customer to come forward and asked for their order. Then she repeated it to me while I took the money.

"One taro tea with black boba," she announced. I scooped up some ice with the jar, added the boba, tea, and taro mixture. Some of the taro mixture dribbled on my shoe. "One strawberry tea, peach popping boba," said Sabrina.

I switched to the strawberry milk. Some of the milk splashed out on my hand. I stopped and got out the wipes I kept with me. Sabrina gave me a nudge. "You can't stop to clean off every time you get some boba on yourself."

"I can't?" This seemed like a horrible idea.

"No, the line is too long, and you're just going to get dirty again. Deal," said Sabrina.

I shuddered and resisted the urge to stop and wipe off my hands. It was just going to be like this, I told myself. No point in cleaning myself off. Just deal. A bee hovered nearby, no doubt attracted to the sweet smell. When Sabrina paused to break a twenty, I quickly cleaned off my hands, but Sabrina was right. One splash just replaced another.

"You're doing great," said Sabrina. I felt like a terrible collage of liquids. Or the sticky floor of a movie theater.

Carly and Jenna came by and got strawberry milk tea with peach boba. "I love this combo," Carly said.

"You definitely told your friends!" said Sabrina, gesturing to the line.

"We told everyone! You should come to all the games. Everyone gets so thirsty." They ordered four more drinks for their friends. I tried to hurry and ended up sloshing taro tea on my pants.

"Ugh!" I tried to move my leg so it wasn't touching the damp fabric. "We should have brought aprons."

"Yeah," admitted Sabrina. "I should have thought about that."

"What if we run out?" I asked. The line didn't seem to be letting up.

"That's the problem we want," said Sabrina. "Once we run out, we gotta go back to your house and make more."

"Today?" All I could think about was a shower. A nice, cleansing shower rinsing away all the stickiness.

"Yes, today! We can make more stuff and run the jars through the dishwasher. We don't have any time to waste. Those Broadway slots are going fast."

"True." I tried to focus on that, and not the sticky patches of boba all over me. After about forty minutes, I told Sabrina we had enough for one last drink. I hadn't stopped to count the money, but by my calculations, we had made at least two hundred dollars. Some people had also given us tips.

I'd told everyone to bring back their jars when they were done, and I also tried to keep an eye on where people had gone to sit. "I'm going to walk around and start collecting jars," I told Sabrina.

"Nah—watch this," she said. She opened a bag in the wagon and called Phinny over. She'd made a harness out of a cloth shoe holder, along with some straps and a sign that said MY NAME IS PHINEAS! RETURN YOUR BOBA JAR TO ME! "Phineas is going to get them for us."

"I'm not sure that's a good idea," I said. I had visions of Phineas running around and bouncing the jars out of the slots, onto the ground. That reminded me of the day Phineas had gotten out of the house. I had Phineas's leash clipped to my belt, and I rechecked it to make sure it was secure.

"Let's find out," said Sabrina. "Give me the leash."

"Shouldn't we at least have a trial run? We can always

just take what we already got back?" I said, but Sabrina just took Phineas toward the stands. People started laughing and calling Phineas over to them. "OMG, so cute," said a girl. "Can he take out the recycling for me?"

"That's next," joked Sabrina. Phineas held still while the girl tucked her jar into the harness. A few more people came over and added their jars. It took a few trips, but it didn't take long to get nearly all the jars back—everyone loved calling to Phineas.

A man walked up to us. "Is that your dog?" he asked, smiling. He stuck his hand out and let Phineas smell it.

Sabrina looked over at me and smirked.

"It's complicated," I said. I looked at Phineas and felt guilty. What if he could understand me? Would he feel bad that I didn't say he was my dog? "Are you looking for a dog?"

"No, no." The man laughed gently and held up an empty mason jar. "I'm here to watch my daughter play. My wife bought one of these from you, and then I saw the dog collecting jars. I'm a local news producer, and you gave me this idea of doing a special on boba tea. This whole thing with the wagon and the dog, it makes a great visual. Fun local interest story."

"You'll put us on TV?" asked Sabrina eagerly. "Like, on the news?"

"Yup. There's a Little League game near here tomorrow night. Maybe you guys could show up there." He handed each of us a business card. It said, *Russell Hayes, On Your Six! Local News.* "How'd you get started in the boba business?"

"We're raising money for a school trip to Broadway," I explained. "For me, that is. Sabrina is helping me. I'm really close to having enough money."

"Oooh, great angle. Viewers love a feel-good story." The man took out a notepad and wrote some things in it. "Do you guys have a name for this?"

"Definitely," I said, surprising myself. I hadn't even talked to Sabrina about it, but the name that popped into my head was just too perfect. "This is Broadway Boba!"

"Broadway Boba," Mr. Hayes repeated. He added that to

his notebook. "Have your parents call me, okay? We could shoot tomorrow, and I'll need to get their permission to have you on air, okay?"

"It's just my dad," I said. Not that he needed to know my life story, but it felt like a lie when people said *parents*, plural, and I didn't correct them.

Mr. Hayes didn't seem fazed. "Then just your dad. No problem."

"Mine will definitely be okay!" said Sabrina as I realized my mistake—I hadn't told Dad about the Broadway trip. Mr. Hayes said he'd be in touch and walked back to the game.

A boy in a baseball cap started to come over. I was about to tell him we were out when Sabrina cried, "Topher!"

"Hey, Sabrina. Hey, Chloe," said Topher. I hadn't recognized him in the hat, which had turned dark with sweat.

"I didn't know you played soccer," said Sabrina. I looked at her, open-mouthed. Sabrina definitely knew Topher played soccer! Topher asked if she wanted to watch some of the next game.

"Sure, if it's okay with Chloe," said Sabrina. She was already handing the leash back to me.

"No problem," I said. I couldn't be mad at Sabrina—she looked too happy. "Aren't humans weird?" I asked Phineas after they walked away. "They start liking someone and they start losing their minds." Phineas wagged his tail. I think he agreed with me!

After I got home from the last game, I counted the money. There was so much money that it was popping out of the shoebox I was keeping it in. I counted it twice to make sure; then I called Sabrina.

"I can't believe how much money we made!" I said. "I'm less than a hundred dollars away from being able to go on the trip." I had made fifty-dollar stacks to keep track. "But we'll have to buy more supplies."

"That's how you'll be able to make more money," Sabrina said.

"True," I admitted. I'd heard Auntie Sue say something

like that. You had to spend money to make money. "Now I just have to tell my dad."

"You were going to have to talk to him anyway," said Sabrina. "Once you had the money to go on the trip. You knew that, right?"

"I suppose." I felt embarrassed that I hadn't planned that far ahead. Wasn't that what I was supposed to be good at?

"Don't make it a big deal," said Sabrina. "Just tell him that the school is having this trip and you raised the money yourself. And then mention the news part."

"It's not that simple," I said.

"Why not?" said Sabrina. "You're paying for the trip." Which sounded a lot more reasonable when it came out of Sabrina's mouth than when it was all in my head.

"Because my dad might feel bad that we don't have the money," I blurted out.

"Would he feel better if he knew you were keeping secrets from him?"

"I wouldn't call it a secret, exactly," I said. "I just don't want him to worry about me."

"You didn't want a mess," said Sabrina. "Like, an emotional one."

"Maybe." I started arranging the money as I talked to Sabrina so the bills all faced the same direction.

"But there are worse things," said Sabrina. "Like feeling someone you love can't ask you for help."

Sabrina, of course, was right. I didn't want Dad to feel that way. "I hate it when you're right," I said.

"You hate it all the time?" said Sabrina, joking.

"How's *Topher*?" I fired back.

"He's fine," said Sabrina. "How's"—and in the small space after that first word, my brain inserted *Henry* and his face popped up in my mind—"going to Broadway feel?" finished Sabrina.

I almost said *How should I know?* but managed to switch at the last second to "It's not a done deal yet. But back to

Topher." *And not Henry.* "Do you like him?" I asked. "And I mean *like* like, just to be clear."

"Maybe," admitted Sabrina. "He's nice."

"I knew it!" I said. "You were being weird."

"Go talk to your dad and quit hassling me!" said Sabrina.

Dad was down in the basement. He was soldering a circuit board, and a tiny plume of smoke rose up. He finished the job and then lifted up his goggles to look at me.

"What's up, kiddo? How was your thing with Sabrina? Did the boba sell well at the restaurant?"

Dad thought we had been making boba for the restaurant? Boba for a taquería? I guess that made sense, at least from his point of view. Why else would we be mass-producing boba tea? I looked at the floor, trying to figure out how to start this conversation. Phineas lay down between us and let out a loud sound, halfway between a moan and moo. He really did seem to know how I felt sometimes.

"Chloe? Is everything okay?" Dad was starting to look worried, which was the last thing I wanted to happen.

"It's fine," I said. *Just say it! You're making it worse!* "So, there's this, uh, trip to Broadway."

"Broadway! As in New York?" said Dad. "That's pretty far."

"I mean, it's a school trip. They have buses and everything. And they do the whole trip in one day," I explained. "But it's kind of expensive."

"Oh, okay." My dad's eyes were sad and kind. I made a wish in my heart that Dad wouldn't be upset.

"So you know how Sabrina and I made a ton of boba?" I asked. "Well, it was to make money for the trip. I've made almost enough money to pay for the whole thing."

"What?" Dad smiled. "That's amazing!" He put his arm around me. "Look at you. A young entrepreneur."

"There's more," I said. "Sabrina came up with this idea to use Phineas to collect the empty jars, and a TV news guy saw us. He wants to do a news spot about us tomorrow with Phineas and everything. If it's okay with you," I added quickly. "Sabrina says I'll probably have enough money for the trip after we're on TV."

I felt Dad's arm loosen. He squinted his eyes, like he was trying to see something far away. "Chloe, are you worried about money again?"

"No, like I said, I'll have enough money for the trip—"

"Not for the trip," interrupted Dad. "I mean in general. For us. We talked about this."

The room seemed to go very still. I nodded my head, just barely. Dad sighed and leaned against his workbench. His head drooped down. This was what I was afraid of.

"Money is not for you to worry about," said Dad. He gestured toward the computer. "Look, I have some work here, for a client."

"But I do," I said. "I do worry about money."

"I'm the parent," said Dad. "That's my job. I want you to be a kid." Dad put his head in his hands. "I don't want that relationship where the parent is always right and says what goes, but I do want you to be a kid."

"I didn't want you to stress out about having enough money for a school trip that is optional," I explained.

"Chloe, things are not what they were," Dad said. "But it's all manageable, okay? We have money for a school trip."

"We do?" I was surprised. "It's almost four hundred dollars."

It was Dad's turn to look surprised. "I—I mean, it's not something that would happen all the time," he stammered. "But we could do it. You need to talk to me."

"Okay," I promised.

"I feel like a bad parent when you worry so much," said Dad. "That's why I got you Phineas. Which . . . also turned out to be a bad idea."

This was news to me. "You got Phineas so I would worry *less*?"

"I got Phineas so you could be a kid," said Dad. "A kid with a dog. But I should have figured you're not a typical kid."

"I like Phineas," I said, giving Dad a hug. "He just makes . . ." I tried to find the right word. "Luàn qī bā zāo."

That was the phrase my mom used when things were disorganized; it always seemed to express the jumble of messiness better than any word in English.

Dad tilted his head back and laughed. "Maybe that's what you need."

"How can anyone need a mess?" I asked while pushing my hands into Phinny's fur. There was something so oddly calming about Phineas, even though he could send me into a panic.

"Maybe Phinny is a marvelous mess," said Dad. "That's the news for tonight. Local dog makes messes but still a good boy." Phineas raised his head when we said his name, tilting it to one side.

"Does that mean we can be on the news?" I asked.

"Yes, but we're going to work on these worries you have," said Dad. "You, kid. Me, adult. Phineas, dog." Then Dad picked up the phone and called Mr. Hayes. That's when it hit me. This was really going to happen!

"Are we still on?" I asked. *It wouldn't be terrible if we weren't,* said my little voice. For once, we were in agreement, me and my little voice.

"Yup," said Dad. "He's really excited. He said it's a perfect spring story with baseball and boba. And a big dog."

"Did Mr. Hayes say what questions he was going to ask?" I said. If I knew the questions ahead of time, I could practice the answers. And not say things like *flatulent.*

"I'm sure it's going to be easy," said Dad. "It's not like an investigation into the dark side of boba, or something."

"I'd still like to know the questions ahead of time," I said. For some reason, Dad thought that was funny!

Getting Taped

By the time I got to school the next day, I discovered that Sabrina had told half the school about the TV thing. And that half seemed to be telling the other half!

"I don't think you should have told so many people," I told Sabrina after we were interrupted at lunch for the fourth time by a group of kids who had heard the news. "We're not going to make that much boba."

"It's a big deal!" said Sabrina, which just made me more nervous. "We're going to be on television. And you know, sometimes national stations pick up stories from local stations. Maybe we'll get on national news!" She put her hand over her mouth and burped. "Excuse me."

I looked around the hallway, scanning for Henry. I wondered if he had heard about us. And what he thought. Did he care? Did I care if he cared?

"Hellloooo? Earth to Chloe! What are you thinking about?" asked Sabrina.

"Oh! Uh, the questions." Thank goodness I had something else I was pre-worrying about. "You'll answer all the questions, right?"

"Oh, come on. You're the reason why we're doing this. They will want to talk to you!"

"Fiiine. I will." I got out a piece of notebook paper. "We should write down some things we'll say tonight, to the news guy."

"You can't hold a piece of paper while you're on TV. That will look stupid," said Sabrina. "You just have to act natural."

"What? I am terrible at improv. Flatulence, remember? I can memorize some basic sentences."

"You can practice some general questions, but you don't want to memorize the answers. You'd look like a robot. Look, if you mess up, you can always have a do-over."

"You can?" I hadn't thought of that. "I mean I can?"

"Oh yeah. Even the news people, they make mistakes all the time and reshoot. Don't worry," said Sabrina. "You'll be great. Besides, those news pieces are usually pretty short. We'll only get a sentence or two. They'll make a little clip with voice-overs and stuff."

"How do you know so much about TV news?" I asked.

"When my parents' first restaurant was on the news, remember?" said Sabrina. She put a fist over her mouth, trying not to burp. "I remember my mom making all sorts of mistakes because she was nervous, but when it aired, there were no mistakes."

"Oh, okay," I said. "That's good. Still, if I start to freeze up, you'll take over, right? Like, what if a ton of people are watching?"

Will Henry be watching? asked my little voice.

Sabrina rolled her eyes. "Oh, come on. These guys aren't going to show up. It's just parents during a midweek Little League game," she said. "Not exactly a sellout crowd, but enough to make money for the trip." She grinned and rubbed her hands together. "Broadway, here we come!"

"But you have to come over to help me make stuff," I said. "After school."

"That's the plan," said Sabrina. She burped again. "Excuse me!" She thumped her fist against her chest. "Gotta tell Mom to go easy on the chilies!"

.•.• 🥤 •.•.

As soon as I got home from school, I got out the pots to start making more strawberry and taro milk. Dad had gone to the store for me during the day to get the ingredients. I started steeping tea and soaking the boba, but I wanted to make the popping boba with Sabrina. I looked at the clock. Sabrina was supposed to be here over half an hour ago.

I called her. Sabrina answered in a faint whisper, "I was just about to call you."

"What's going on?" She sounded terrible.

"We got food poisoning," said Sabrina. "Mom said we must have gotten a bad batch of fish or something. We're all here fighting over who gets the bathroom . . . No, Mamá, not the tea." I could hear Sabrina's mom arguing with her. "My mom wants me to drink this terrible-tasting tea."

"Oh no! I'm so sorry." I meant the whole thing, feeling sick and having to drink terrible tea. "Maybe I'll call the news guy . . ."

"No," said Sabrina. Her voice grew stronger. "You just have to deal. You can do it. You need to raise the money by yourself now."

I tried to quell the panic rising in my throat. "But we're a team," I said.

"I'll be there in spirit," said Sabrina. There was a long pause. "Gotta go!" The phone suddenly clicked off.

I turned to Phineas. "What am I going to do? I still have to make the popping boba, and pour the drinks, and . . ."

You didn't think this would actually work, did you? asked my little voice. I shook my head. I was going to make this work. Phineas looked at me and sighed. Then he got up and scratched at the door leading to Dad's workshop. Maybe he was trying to get away from me, but it seemed like a sign.

I walked over to the door and shouted down the stairs, "Dad! I need your help!"

Dad helped me make more popping boba and pour the drinks into serving containers. Then he drove me and Phineas over to the field with the drinks. "Sorry I can't stay," said Dad as he took the wagon out of the trunk of the car. "I'm on a deadline. But you've got this, Chloe."

I gave Dad a hug. "I'll manage."

Phineas pulled on his leash and barked happily. Then I

heard someone yell, "They're here!" I stared at the throngs of people hanging around the dugouts and along the chain-link fence that encircled the field. There were parents, but there were also lots of kids from our school. I even spotted a few teachers.

"Nobody's going to show up, huh?" I said to Phineas.

A white van with a blue ON YOUR SIX! logo pulled into the parking lot. Mr. Hayes jumped out of the passenger side and waved.

"Sabrina couldn't make it!" I shouted. Suddenly, I had this thought that telling Mr. Hayes that Sabrina wasn't there would make him jump back into the van and drive away. But he didn't seem bothered. Or maybe he didn't hear me. He just called, "Start selling! We'll get some footage, and then we'll come interview you."

A crowd was heading my way. I was starting to wish I'd been the one to get food poisoning. How was I going to manage? *This is going to be a disaster, and it's going to be on the news.* Phineas whined and barked.

Maybe I could have people just drop the money in the box while I made their drinks. That would make one task easier. And I could remind them to bring back the jar. If more people did that, then I wouldn't have to spend more time taking Phinny to retrieve them. But Mr. Hayes probably would want some action shots of Phineas getting the jars.

I started to put the apron on, but then remembered I should clip Phinny's leash to my belt first. In the confusion of taking the apron back off, the leash slipped off my hand. That was enough for Phineas. He took off, running toward the crowd of people.

"Phineas! Come back!" I shouted. At least Phinny wasn't running toward the road. He wanted to meet the new people, and they weren't coming fast enough. I could see his tail wagging furiously.

"You bad dog!" I said. I hated leaving the wagon full of supplies, but Phineas wasn't coming back to me. He was wading farther into the crowd. I marched after him. "Come back here!" I didn't want to yell at Phineas in a mean way, but I was starting to feel it. This was the last thing I needed! "Can somebody grab the leash?" I called. I couldn't see Phineas, but I could see people moving around him. I looked back at the wagon. I hoped no one would get the idea to help themselves to the drinks!

Phineas's face popped back out of the crowd. He was smiling, his pink tongue hanging out, as though he had done something to be proud of. Part of me wanted to hug him; the other part wanted to strangle him. He was not helping! I reached to grab his leash, but someone was holding it.

Henry. Henry was at the other end of the leash.

I could feel the corners of my mouth start to go up. *I'm not smiling because Henry's here. I'm just glad that I have Phineas back*, I told myself, before my little voice got any ideas. *That's it.*

"I think your dog needs obedience lessons," said Henry, handing over the leash. His eyes were shining with amusement. He probably thought it was funny that Phineas was causing me so much trouble. Phineas could not be put into an orderly pile.

"Thanks," I said shortly. "I'll add that to my to-do list." I looked away while I talked so I wouldn't have to look at his dimple.

Henry didn't leave. "Where's your partner in crime? You guys are, like, inseparable."

"Sabrina isn't feeling well," I said. "I gotta do this solo."

Henry gestured toward my apron. "You got another one of those? I can help."

"You don't have to," I said while trying to shush the little voice cheering in my head. *Help has arrived! And it's Henry the Boba Master!* "I've got this."

My little voice started booing me. *Why are you being so dumb, Chloe?*

"Chloe, I know how this works. There's no way you can do this yourself and not look like a hot mess on television. There's a reason why we have multiple people working at Tea Palace."

I sighed. *This* was a mess. I was supposed to be mad at Henry, but here I was, a tiny bit glad to see him. I crossed my arms, trying to remember how to be mad at him. "What are you even doing here?" I asked. "Did you know that Phineas was going to break loose again?"

"Actually, I was told to come find you," said Henry slowly. He held up his phone and pushed a button. Henry's uncle . . . and Auntie Sue appeared on the screen. What was happening?

"Is that Chloe?" Auntie Sue peered at the screen.

"Yes, it's me and Henry," I said. Henry stood next to me so we would both be on the screen together.

"Perfect! Chloe! We have something to tell you! Martin proposed!" Auntie Sue said.

Auntie Sue was shouting at her usual volume, but the words didn't make any sense. "Proposed what? A business proposal?" Was there going to be a second Tea Palace?

"No, silly!" She held up her hand. She was wearing a sparkly diamond ring! "We got engaged!" Henry's uncle had the biggest, dopiest grin on his face.

The crowd around us was starting to build up, but I was too astonished to start making boba. "Congratulations!" I said. "But I thought you guys were mad at each other."

"We talked," said Auntie Sue.

"A lot," added Henry's uncle, who was now, I supposed, about to be my uncle Martin.

"You're not mad anymore?" I asked.

Henry jumped in. "They had started explaining that my grandfather had sent my uncle away because he wanted him to focus on his studies, not have a girlfriend."

"That's why he suddenly went AWOL?!" I said. "That's bananas."

"He got sent away to Singapore to study," said Henry. "Anyway, they said I had to come find you, like the olden days, so you could be part of the conversation. I told them that everyone at Roosevelt Middle School knew where you were right now."

Uncle Martin gave me a lopsided smile. "My grades started to go downhill when I met Sue. My father said I had to focus on my studies."

"But he never forgot me," said Auntie Sue, squeezing his

arm. "But he should have told me what was happening!" She play-slapped his arm.

"I didn't want to say goodbye. It would have been too hard. I'm so lucky I wasn't too late," said Uncle Martin. "Not too late for a second chance." Now they were practically ending each other's sentences.

"We're starting over," said Auntie Sue. "Doing all the things we should have done."

"A wedding. A honeymoon," said Uncle Martin.

"A dog! We're getting a dog!" added Auntie Sue.

"Whatever she wants," said Uncle Martin. He leaned over and gave Auntie Sue a big smooch on the cheek.

"Who is this man, and what did he do to my uncle?" muttered Henry under his breath as he clicked off his phone.

We both stared at the empty screen. "That's . . . amazing," I said.

"I thought she was going to beat him up the last time I saw them," said Henry.

"I think that was the other possibility," I said. "I'm glad they talked first."

Henry laughed. "He'd been acting so strangely around the store. Now it all makes sense." I reminded myself that Henry had come here because his uncle had told him to, not because he wanted to help me. Maybe he was still mad at me.

I looked around us. "I really do need to get going on this boba tea thing. But you don't have to help. I can do it."

"Look," said Henry. "I said some dumb things, like, really dumb things I didn't mean, because I thought you had gotten your boba from another store. I'm sorry. Let me help? I really want to. I want to help you get to Broadway."

"Which you hate."

"I never said I hated it," said Henry. "I just said I thought it was fake. But I watched a few movies . . ."

"You did?" I was surprised. "Like what?"

"Um, lessee. *Singing' in the Rain. West Side Story. Come from Away.* I even watched some Bollywood musicals. With the subtitles." I had to admit, I was impressed.

"I figured out something," said Henry.

The first kid in line interrupted. "Are you guys going to talk all day, or are you actually going to serve us?"

"How can I help you?" asked Henry. He turned to me. "What flavors do we have, anyway?"

"Strawberry and taro milk tea," I said. "Black boba and peach popping boba."

"Very popular drinks," observed Henry. The kid asked for strawberry milk tea with black boba. Henry took the money and handed me a jar with ice and black boba. I added the strawberry milk and tea.

It seemed almost surreal that Henry was helping me with boba. After saying that Broadway was fake. Even though he worked at an actual boba place. I tried to think of something to say. "So, Henry the Boba Master, if Thai tea is the drink to have when I have to organize my notebook for Mr. McRyan, what is strawberry milk tea good for?" I asked.

Henry didn't say anything for a long time, so long I

207

thought maybe he hadn't heard me. Then he said, without looking at me, "Hanging out with someone nice on a spring day."

What? Did Henry *like* like me? Did I *like* like Henry? And wasn't that the ultimate mess, *like* liking someone? Auntie Sue and Uncle Martin had been through an ultimate mess, and now here they were, smiling and happy. Maybe Henry just wanted to be friends—that would be okay, wouldn't it?

Would it be okay with me? What if I made a mess?

I focused on making the drinks so I wouldn't have to listen to the thoughts swirling in my head.

.•.• 🧋 •.•.

"Broadway or bust? That's what this young lady decided when she began selling the popular Asian drink, boba, as a way of raising money for the trip." Mr. Hayes was speaking to the camera, standing slightly in front of me. Henry declined to be on camera, so he stood behind Mr. Hayes, watching the camera. "How's business today? What's popular?"

"Business is good. One of our favorite drinks is, uh,

strawberry milk tea with . . ." My mind was going blank. What was it called?

Henry made fireworks motions with his hands.

"Oh! With, uh, exploding boba."

"Exploding boba?" Mr. Hayes looked confused.

Henry shook his head and mouthed something. I tried to lip read. "Bobbing baba! Boba boba." Henry bent over and made the letter *P* with his body. "No, popping boba! Peaching pop poppa. Peach popping boba." I took a deep breath. "Can I have a do-over?"

Mr. Hayes smiled. "I'll pitch you the question again. How's business today? What's popular?"

"Our strawberry milk tea with popping peach boba . . ." I said that part very slowly and carefully. ". . . is selling really well."

"Tell me about the glass jars."

"The glass jars seemed like a good way to make us stand out and to help the environment," I said. That one went better. Henry gave me a thumbs-up.

"Now, at your stand, you have two flavors, taro and straw-berry, and two add-ins, black boba and the popping boba," said Mr. Hayes. "Some people are telling us they like the limited selection, because too many choices are confusing. What do you say to that?"

Whoa, I wasn't expecting that one. "Well, um, the reason why we have a limited selection, um . . ." Why *did* we have a limited selection? "Oh, we, um, couldn't buy all the flavors," I said. I sounded like a moron! I looked over at Henry. "But if you do go somewhere, like Tea Palace, there are people who can help you figure out what you like."

And there are people you just plain like at Tea Palace.

Focus, Chloe!

"Tell us about the dog. How does the dog help run your business?" asked Mr. Hayes. I noticed Mr. Hayes said *the* dog, not *your* dog.

"Phineas here collects the jars so we can wash and reuse them. People love interacting with Phineas. He's trouble sometimes, but he's a good boy." Suddenly, the words came out easily. I wasn't stumbling or mixing up my words, maybe because they were so true. I ruffled Phineas's fur.

It was true that Phineas was a fur-covered disaster. He had nearly cost me my grade in social studies, and he'd freaked me out when he ran into the street.

He also had an expression that zoomed straight to my heart, and when I needed help, Phineas was the one who helped me figure it out. Sometimes, just petting him made me feel better. Maybe sometimes a marvelous mess wasn't an event—it was a dog.

I didn't want Phineas to go. And all I had to do was say yes.

"He's *my* good boy," I said, in a slightly louder voice. Suddenly, the relief I thought I would feel by letting go of Phineas came rushing out when I decided to keep him. I put my arms around Phineas. "This giant, jar-collecting dog is mine!" Phineas tilted his head and licked my face.

"Okay, now one last question, and some footage of your dog getting the jars back," said Mr. Hayes. "Have you made enough money for your trip?" he asked.

I counted the remaining jars. "I have." Suddenly, it hit me. I was actually going to Broadway! It wasn't a dream anymore. "I'm going to Broadway!"

"Here's one more sale!" said Mr. Hayes, handing me a five-dollar bill. He smiled and winked. "Now that's a nice ending."

"The real ending is when I'm on my way to the Gershwin Theatre next month!" I said. I looked around. "Wait. Where's Henry? Where'd he go?"

"The kid?" asked the cameraman. "He said he had to go back to work."

"I passed him on the way here." It was Mrs. Alamantia! She smiled at me and held out her hands. "You worked so hard, Chloe," she said. I grabbed her hands and squeezed.

"Did you come to buy a drink?" I asked her. "We have a little bit of both left, no popping boba, though. But I have enough money for the trip!"

"There are six spots left," said Mrs. Alamantia. "And one of them is yours as long as you bring in your money and form tomorrow. First thing!"

"Last I heard there were seven," I said. "I guess I'm getting mine in just in time."

"You don't know?" asked Mrs. A. "You don't know who just got the other spot?"

"No," I said. "Why would I?"

"Huh," said Mrs. A mysteriously. "I guess you don't keep tabs on everything as well as I thought you did."

17

Sticky Hands

I sent a text to Sabrina, telling her the good news. Then Phineas and I walked home with the wagon. *My dog*, Phineas, and I walked home. How did everything seem so right when it seemed like the worst possible decision?

"I did it!" I told Dad when I got home. "I sold the boba and did the news thing without being completely terrible. I did need one do-over," I conceded. Suddenly, the image of Henry contorting himself into the letter *P* leapt into my head, and I laughed out loud.

"I knew you could do it," said Dad. "Can't wait to see the news piece!" I gave Dad a hug, and Phineas spun around us, his tail swishing our legs. "Sweet Caroline" was playing on the stereo again, but I didn't feel sad this time. "Working on a new project?"

"I'm still trying to figure out how to get K-99 to teach heeling. Make Phineas more appealing to a new family," said Dad. "The family that visited didn't work out, partly because they weren't sure they could handle a big dog."

"He's definitely a lot of dog." I took a deep breath. "I have a better idea. Let's keep Phineas and teach him ourselves."

"What? Whoa," said Dad. "Are you sure?" Even as he asked, though, a smile started to spread across Dad's face.

Was I sure? I looked around the room, with the three of us in it, with "Sweet Caroline" on the stereo, and realized that maybe this was what was missing. The house was never going to be like it was with Mom, but we could still have love, just a different kind, with different people and creatures. And happiness. And mistakes.

"I'm sure," I said.

"Well," said Dad. "That's great!" He leaned over and scratched Phineas behind the ears. "Did you hear that, Phineas?"

"Did you also hear that Phineas is getting a . . . ?" I tried to figure out what the relationship would be between Phineas and the dog that Auntie Sue and Uncle Martin were going to get. I gave up. "A cousin?"

Dad didn't know. I gave him the whole rundown, what happened at the park. Everything that happened once I let things get . . . slightly out of control.

"Maybe we'll have to have them over for dinner," said Dad. "Your mother would have liked that."

"We can finally figure out how to make the Three Cup Chicken the way Mom did," I said. "Auntie Sue can help."

"I'd like that," said Dad. "We don't even have to do it on a Thursday."

My head seemed to buzz with the slightly unknown. But instead of being scary, it felt like possibility. And there was one more possibility, one more mess, I couldn't let go.

"I made some extra money," I told Dad. "I think I'm going to go get a boba tea."

"Really? Aren't you sick of boba?" asked Dad.

"Apparently not," I told him.

I tried not to run to Tea Palace. Be cool. Maybe I was wrong. Maybe I was misreading the whole situation. But I had to find out.

The store was getting ready to close. Henry was mopping the floor, and someone else was emptying out the trash can. Maybe I was too late. Maybe it was the wrong time. Maybe I'd say the wrong thing. Before I could turn around, though, Henry spotted me through the glass and waved me in.

"I thought you'd be sick of boba by now," said Henry, smiling.

"I'm not tired of someone else making boba," I said.

Henry swept his hand toward the menu board. "What would you like?"

What did you order when you were about to open your

heart and let everything out? Maybe something that turned you into an amnesiac so if everything went wrong, you could forget about it.

"Oh." This was scary. "Before I order, uh, you had started to say something, right before we started selling boba. About the thing you had figured out about musicals." *Are those even sentences?* asked my little voice. *Is there a coherent thought in there?*

"I did?" Henry looked up at the ceiling, his mouth twisting. I wanted to keep looking at that face. And listening to what Henry had to say. "Let's go sit down," said Henry. We went to the table near the middle of the restaurant, hidden by the bamboo.

"This is where Sabrina and I sat, the first day we came in," I said.

"I remember," said Henry. "You sat there." He pointed at me. "And Sabrina sat here."

Was it weird that Henry remembered? Was it weird that

I remembered seeing Henry's dimple for the first time on that day?

"So, um, did I tell you that I'm going on the Broadway trip?" asked Henry.

"No!" That must have been what Mrs. A was talking about. "Is that what you were going to tell me?"

Henry looked away. "I'll take care of cleaning up," he said to a boy who had started to mop near us. "Don't worry about it." Henry waited until the boy moved away.

Then he looked at me steadily and said, "No, Chloe. That's not what I was going to tell you."

Your nose has a boog . . . started my little voice. And then it shut up because Henry was looking at me.

I thought about what Mrs. A said. That there was nothing more amazing than that moment in the theater right before the curtain went up, just before everything begins.

We weren't in a theater. We were in a boba shop. But it felt the same.

Henry bent his head down as if he were studying the tabletop. "Here goes," he said. "I figured out that even though musicals are fake . . ."

I shook my head slightly. I thought Henry would miss seeing it, but he lifted his head just in time.

"Even though musicals are undoubtedly the fakest thing on earth, faker than blue sports drinks and pizza with weird stuff in the crust, the thing about musicals is that . . ." Henry paused. "The way they make you feel is real."

The whole room seemed to become a spotlight. And that spotlight was on us.

"How do they make you feel?" I asked, keeping my voice low.

"They make me feel the way I feel when I'm with you, Chloe," said Henry, looking at me steadily. "Maybe I feel like I don't need musicals, because when I'm with you, I already feel like I'm in one."

This was a mess. A big uncontrollable mess. *Like* like. But what did Sabrina say? Some things were worse than messes. And maybe some things were better than messes. Like Phineas. Like making up. Like this.

Henry put his hand over mine. I liked the way it felt.

"My hands are sticky," said Henry. "Sorry. You probably hate that."

"Occupational hazard," I said. "I totally get it."

He let go of my hand for a second to reach for a napkin. "I made a matcha tea right before you came in. I can make my hands less sticky."

I pushed the napkin away and put my hand over his. "I don't mind being stuck," I said. And then I held his hand a little tighter.

"What's the best boba drink for when you finally tell someone how much you like them?" I asked.

Henry smiled. "I've been waiting to make that drink for a long time. Come on."

Acknowledgments

Thank you as always to my editor, Lisa Sandell, for suggesting that I write a light romance/boba story. It turns out that writing a rom-com is almost as fun as watching/reading one! Many thanks to my partner in crime, Madelyn Rosenberg, and my agent, Tracey Adams. My world is bubblier with you all in it.

About the Author

Wendy Wan-Long Shang is the author of *The Great Wall of Lucy Wu*, which was awarded the Asian/Pacific American Librarians Association Award for Children's Literature; *The Way Home Looks Now*, an Amelia Bloomer Project List selection and a CCBC *Choices* List selection; *The Secret Battle of Evan Pao*, a *Washington Post* Summer Book Club pick; Sydney Taylor Honor Book *This Is Just a Test*, which she cowrote with Madelyn Rosenberg; *Not Your All-American Girl*, a *Tablet* Magazine Best Children's Book, also cowritten with Madelyn Rosenberg; and *The Rice in the Pot Goes Round and Round*. She lives with her family in the suburbs of Washington, DC.

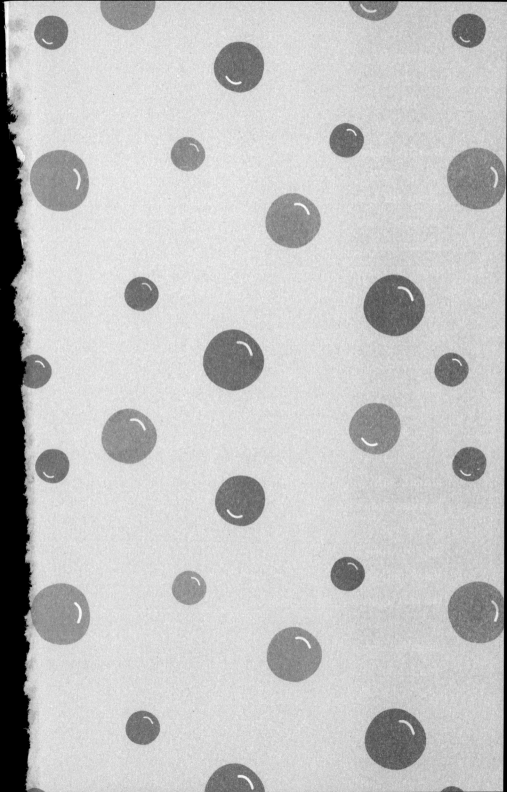

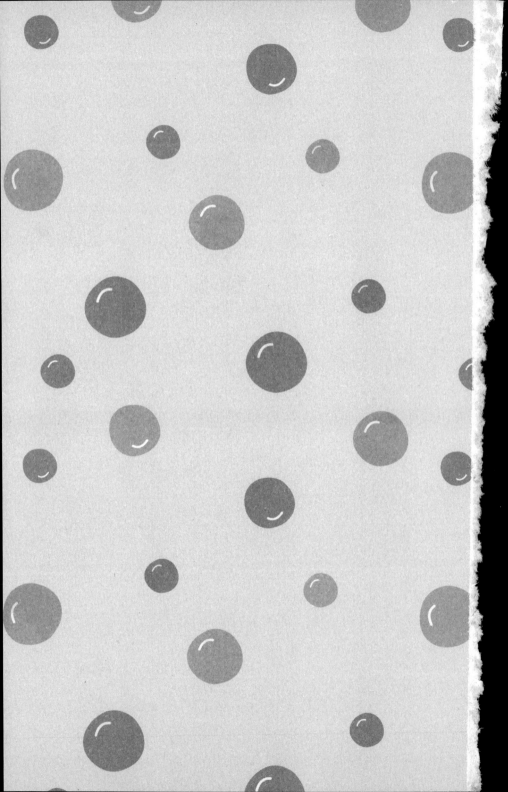